Alpha & Omega

K WEBSTER

Cover Design: K. Webster
Photo: Dollar Photo Club
Editor: Mickey Reed
Formatting: Champagne Formats

ISBN-13: 978-1507856925
ISBN-10: 150785692X

Dedication

To my very own Alpha,
'Til death.
And even after I take my last breath.
I promise you forever.
Your very own Twiggy

But our love it was stronger by far than the love
Of those who were older than we—
Of many far wiser than we—
And neither the angels in Heaven above
Nor the demons down under the sea
Can ever dissever my soul from the soul
Of the beautiful Annabel Lee;

~An excerpt from Annabel Lee by Edgar Allan Poe~

Prologue

LIFE IS NOTHING but a sequential series of monotonous repeats. You wake up and then you eat. You work and then you eat. You bathe and then you eat. Oh, and then you sleep.

Over.

And.

Fucking over again.

Life is a blur. Each passing moment is just another second closer to your final destination—six feet under the dirt to be mourned and eventually forgotten.

I wasn't made for life. Unfortunately, I was one of the few who figured out the algorithms of this godforsaken planet and became a slave to the monotony. I knew my ultimate destiny was death. The overdramatic poet in me craved that end, because maybe then I could actually feel something besides the constant internal clock counting each second until my expiration. My thought was: Let's hurry and get this phase of my existence over with so that I can move the fuck on. Life is like the lobby of a doctor's office. Or waiting to get your driver's license renewed at the DMV.

Boring.

As.

Fuck.

Each day, I toyed with the idea of speeding the process up. Sure, I lived in a home with lovely parents who bought me lovely things and loved me dearly. But something was missing inside me—that little part that keeps everyone else grounded and emotionally tied to this Earth. For me, that part was void. It never existed in the first place, so I hadn't been able to grow or nurture it like everyone else. In me, there were no feelings of hope or excitement. I did not envision children or a spouse or a kickass career.

All I could think about was what color the inside of my coffin would be. Would my parents splurge and get me a ridiculous silk–lined, wooden box that caused them to tap into their retirement? Or would they just use their credit card and buy the midgrade one—the one that has a thin padding and scratchy material but looks good enough on the outside?

I didn't plan on staying there anyway. They could have cremated me if that had been more in their budget. I'd have been happy with my remains sitting on the mantel next to Granny's and our dog, Buckie. It honestly wouldn't have mattered because I figured I would be running full force into the afterlife that awaited me. Something deep inside me knew I was better mentally equipped for that next phase. A part of me twitched and fidgeted at the idea of what was to come.

Was that what these other brainless drones called hope?

Dare I say I was hopeful?

Then it was all ruined.

One smile. One goddamned beautiful smile infected my heart and soul with such a force that I nearly exploded. All hopes of afterlife and the eagerness to leave this one vanished with that one handsome smile.

Thump.

My heart gave one painful thud and began beating for the first time in its life. I hated the feeling. Hated that the powers that be had realized I was onto their game. They made me their project. They showed me a smile. I was diseased by light from such a simple gesture.

Surely I could manage to look away and remember my goals. There had to be a way to avoid the magnetic glow that sucked me right in.

And then he spoke.

The beautiful smile had an even more beautiful voice. And with each word, each joke, and, eventually, each touch, I intertwined my soul so intricately with his that I never had a chance of letting go.

I fell in love.

And suddenly, life wasn't long enough.

Chapter One

Alpha

TODAY IS FA day—the day when all of us Minders take on our final assignments before advancing to Seraph Guardians and getting our wings. I've wanted to be an SG since the moment I was recruited to HEA Corp.

Six years ago, I woke up with no recollection of my past. I'd been killed or died in some traumatic way but had "heroic qualities" according to my recruiting officer, Pallas, which is why I was recruited by HEA. That day, I showed up alongside Omega. They partnered us up, and we've been inseparable ever since.

Minders like Omega and I don't need sleep. We don't require any sustenance like food and water. Minders also don't care about love or hate, right or wrong. Those of us who find ourselves in this position care about one thing: protecting those fragile, earthly beings they call humans. Since we were also human at one time, being a Minder is the step before becoming the ultimate badass, an SG. All Minders strive to become SGs. Unfortunately, not all Minders become them. Sometimes, they can't cut it and are sent next door for work.

Most Minders take decades to complete their assignments because they either fail or get more assignments as more required training. Omega and I, like a well-oiled wheel, are like the Tango and Cash of the afterlife. Our assignments come easily to us, and we have a great time completing them. When on assignment, we work together like two halves of a whole, which is why we're kicking ass and taking names. The other Minders, especially Herra and Loper, are jealous bastards, but they can't do a damn thing about it. And if they get too mouthy, HEL Enterprises is always at our doorsteps looking for new hires.

Omega and I often converse to see if we were brothers or best friends in our prior human bodies, but neither of us can remember and Pallas refuses to tell us. It only makes sense that we knew each other. Two people can't be that close upon instant meeting. There was a bond and a deep trust neither of us could pinpoint the origin to. Regardless, we held on to that bond and strengthened it over the past six years. I'd die for Omega—*if* I could die, that is.

The biggest downfall of becoming a Minder is the memory loss. You wake up in a body that doesn't belong to you, talking in a voice that was never yours, with a blank memory. For most, it isn't a big deal. Omega gives me shit about caring who the old me was. Something in my brain, though, won't allow me to give up. It is against our laws to discover who we were, and we aren't supposed to try. But I'll always wonder. And when I become an SG, I'll have the resources to find out.

"Ready for this, Al?" Omega's voice thunders as we tromp down the marbled hallway sounding like a herd of elephants.

"Brother, I was born ready. Pallas can bring on his toughest shit and I'll handle it with finesse," I joke as I slide my fingers through my longish, inky-black hair.

Omega calls my hair The Chick Magnet. The female Minders in our sector go batshit crazy over my hair. Minders don't care about their own looks. We actually avoid mirrors at all costs. Vanity isn't something we're allowed to think about—seven deadly sins and all—but we do care about the looks of others. Apparently, I'm what the females call "a hottie." Omega tells me all the time that it isn't fair that I got The Chick Magnet hair and he got lame, chocolate curls. He reminds me of a male model I had to once protect on assignment. The females here call Omega dreamy.

Hottie and Dreamy.

We kick ass and we're good-looking motherfuckers too. This life is a pretty sweet one, I tell you.

"Good luck, boys," Lovenia purrs as she stands outside the door of Pallas's office.

Omega lets an animalistic growl loose and I chuckle. Those two have it so bad for each other, but neither is making any steps to move forward. There's so much sexual tension between them that, when they finally do climb into the sack together, both Heaven and Hell will weep with joy because, quite frankly, we're all just over it.

Lovenia is a Leviathan. Try saying that three times fast. She's a higher-up at HEL Enterprises but likes slumming it with us when she's not on assignment. Our buildings are side by side, and our companies are sister companies. Employees of HEA work their way up. Literally. The higher the floor in our building, the more powerful you are at this company. HEL works just the opposite. Their head honcho, Luc, offices in the basement. They tell me it's hot there.

"You don't need luck when you're the Alpha and Omega duo. Luck needs us, baby," I grin and then wink at her.

She blushes and bats those long, dark lashes at me. Lovenia is all curves and smart as a whip, and she will lance you to bits with her sharp Latina tongue. Big, tough Omega will be handcuffed to her bed soon—it's only a matter of time. I may be a huge flirt, but I don't mess around too much on their side. It isn't against the Minder rules, but it is against SG policy. I figure the less I commingle with them, the better. My goals are big, so I can't let anyone or anything stand in my way.

"Hey, Omega. Why don't you come by my place after you get your FA and I'll give you a special treat," she speaks seductively to my partner.

The low growl in his throat is one of pure want. If he wants to fuck her before becoming an SG, that'll be his only chance. I know my boy. He already has her naked in his head.

"I have a treat of my own for you, sweet Love," he smirks back.

She beams beautifully at his nickname for her, and for a second, I wonder if he'll back out on FA day just to haul her back to his quarters. They hold each other's heated stares before she approaches him and pecks him on the cheek.

"I'll be waiting in nothing but a big, red bow tied around my hips. You better hurry back and unwrap your gift," she says in a manner that could bring any man to his knees. Good thing my brother isn't human.

"Move it along, princess. We have work to do," I grumble in faux annoyance.

She giggles all the way down the hallway as she leaves us to take our final assignment before becoming true guardian angels. My mother would be proud—if I actually had one.

Omega strides up to Pallas's door and knocks loudly. Pallas is a partially deaf SG officer. Word on the street is he lost his hearing on his FA before becoming an SG. They don't speak much of their assignments because they are intended to be classified. But, even though we're angels in training, we're not perfect. The gossip mill is a quiet yet powerful machine. It doesn't help that most Leviathans are behind every rumor, whether it be truth or myth.

"Come in," Pallas hollers through the thick, wooden door.

Omega turns the knob and pushes through the opening. Instantly, we're hit with the stench of cigars. Good ol' Pallas has one permanently affixed between his yellow teeth, it would seem. Not once have I ever seen him take it out in the six years I've known him.

"Sit, boys," the gravelly voiced officer instructs.

We sit side by side and eagerly await our assignment. My leg has begun to bounce with contained energy that's just waiting to explode. This time in our life is do or die. We either pass or fail this final assignment. Passing means promotion and wings. Failing means termination from HEA Corp. Failure is not an option because I'd die before ever working for the other side which is exactly what would happen.

"First of all, I want to tell you both how proud of you I am. When I stumbled upon you two, I knew you were special. The both of you are like sons of mine." He takes a minute to let that sink in. "That being said, your final assignment will be difficult. My commanding officers have studied both of your cases and found things to insert into your mission that could compromise your ability to perform. They have direct access to your prior life. Your weaknesses have been highlighted and will be turned against you."

Omega grunts, and I flit my eyes over to him. His dark-brown eyes are brooding. He senses something bad coming. And I'd be a fool if I didn't sense it too.

"We're Minders, not humans. I think we can manage. We've killed it on every other mission, boss. You know this," I tell Pallas. Something in my voice indicates my uncertainty, and I instantly hate that feeling.

Pallas groans as he spouts off his next piece. “Yes, you kept your subjects alive for the allotted time periods before the Reapers took them. That’s to be commended. Neither of you has ever failed. But to be SG worthy, you have to be strong in any capacity.”

So far, our jobs have been easy. They put us on a subject that can’t see or hear us. We watch their every move. When they walk into traffic, we surge our power to make cars brake. If they slip in the shower, we break their fall. A subject of mine once choked on a meatball while at home alone and I just blasted him on the back, hurtling the meat across the room. We protect them—mostly from themselves—until D Day, also known as Death Day.

When Death Day arrives, the minions over at HEL, called Reapers, swoop in and take them to their final destination. Lovenia says that it’s like a vacation at a warm beach minus the water and way hotter. Doesn’t sound too bad . . .

“Did you hear me?” Pallas grumbles, yanking my attention back to him.

Not missing a beat, I say, “So, you’re telling us something changes in the way we do our job?”

“Exactly. Same rules apply as far as mirrors—stay away so you don’t become weak. And in the instance you do become weak, find a church or Bible—you’ll heal quickly.”

Omega and I nod in response. Nothing new so far.

“Here’s the deal, boys,” Pallas groans. “You’ll be human for this job.”

Omega bursts from his chair in a furious blast and leans across the desk with his finger in Pallas’s face. “You can’t do that! We’re about to become fucking guardian angels! What about our powers?”

He’s outraged, and I can’t help but feel slightly betrayed. Why train us one way and then send us out with no tools?

“Don’t curse in my office. I should write you up for that,” Pallas snaps and swats Omega’s hand away.

“Sit down, buddy. We’ll figure it out,” I tell him and yank down on the back of his suit jacket. Then I nervously wipe my palms on the thighs even though I don’t sweat. Must be an old habit from my prior life.

Once Omega has relaxed a bit in his chair, Pallas continues his instructions.

"You won't have your powers. In fact, by becoming human for that short time, you'll be susceptible to real-life inflictions that will carry over to when you are an SG or . . ." he trails off.

We know he means we'll become fucking Reapers if we don't pass this mission.

"Anyway," he continues, "that's how I got this hearing problem. Bar fight. Some prick hit me in the head with a barstool while I was trying to protect a pool shark I was in charge of. You can get injured, but you won't die. You're still immortal. But don't go getting your legs blown off or some wicked stuff like that. You'll be a worthless SG. Believe me—I had to prove my tail off that I could still be an SG even with a handicap. That, boys, is why I sit behind a desk versus being out there with the likes of you."

My mind spins at what he's telling us. Omega is boiling over with rage.

"So, we'll be stripped of our powers, visible to our charges, and faced with obstacles we struggled with while in our former human lives? How long are our assignments?" I question.

Where Omega is pissed, I'm impatient to get this started. Something deep within me bounces back and forth on each foot like a boxer eager to fight. I love challenges, and thus far, we've handled everything with ease. Nobody has died on either of our watches. HEL got their people and we got closer to becoming an SG.

"In a nutshell. You'll encounter some other 'obstacles' along the way—and by 'obstacles,' I mean a Leviathan will be assigned to the both of you to complicate things. Why do you think Lovenia was here?" he grumbles as if her very existence makes him cringe.

To the both of us?

"Wait. You said, 'To the both of us.' We're always in close proximity for our missions, but you make it sound like we'll be on the same one," I say slowly.

"What happens if Lovenia fails in distracting us?" Omega spouts out, interrupting me.

His sudden interest in her well-being frays my nerves a bit, but I try to ignore it. Omega is the more passionate of the two of us. I'm the level head and the final say. In the end, Omega always listens to me.

"Yes. Your missions are neighbors in an apartment building. You'll be staying in the apartment across the hall from them. And, Omega, Lovenia's superiors will handle her failures—it isn't anything for you to think twice about. Here are your files," he says, handing us each a thick, brown folder.

I open mine and see a black and white photo of a dark-haired woman with hollow, drug-hazed eyes paper clipped to the front. She's beautiful but lost, hence her making it onto an FA list. Only the truly fucked up get on our list. As I skim through her file, I look at the assignment duration—three months. All of our other assignments have been less than a month. The length of time unnerves me.

"Why so long?" Omega growls out his question, mimicking my internal one.

Pallas sighs, "Just part of the challenge. Look, boys, if it were easy, everyone would be a Seraph Guardian. The good people of this Earth deserve to be protected by angels who don't fall into temptation, are strong during moments of weakness, and don't become attached. This is your final test. You've passed with flying colors thus far. Granted, you will be pushed, but the two of you are strong. You'll succeed—I know it. I wouldn't have recruited you otherwise."

I flop my file closed and look over at my angry partner, who has his own file clutched so tight that his knuckles are turning white.

"Anything else, boss?" I ask Pallas while keeping my eyes trained on Omega.

"Report back here weekly. Look out for each other. And, boys," he says gruffly, "make me proud."

Why do I feel as if this will be more difficult than either of us could ever imagine?

Chapter Two

Lark

THE THUMP OF my neighbor's bass infuriates me as I stalk toward my apartment door after a long-ass shift at the tattoo shop. All I want to do is crawl into my bed and pass out. I dealt with a whiny-ass biker earlier who was at least six foot three and nearly three hundred pounds for five hours straight as I inked his ribs with the words "Badass Motherfucker" encased in a bed of skulls. The pussy cried while his biker bitch stroked his hair. I wanted to fucking puke, but I was making five hundred bucks on the deal and needed it to support my habit.

My habit.

The only thing that makes me smile in this godforsaken life.

I pull the keys from my worn purse and prepare to push them into the lock when I hear the music getting louder as Pedro emerges from his apartment.

Fuck.

"*Estás muy buena!*" he hollers as he stumbles his way toward me.

"Not tonight, asshole. I'm tired as hell, and for the thousandth time, I'm not going to sleep with you," I snarl as I whirl around to face him.

He's totally fucked up tonight, which sends a shiver skittering down my spine. I can hardly thwart his advances on a normal night, but when he's high on meth, it's nearly impossible because he is so damn persistent.

I attempt to turn the key in the lock with my eyes watching his every move. I'm not letting him out of my sight until the door slams in his face and I'm safely behind my locked front door.

"*Chupame la polla,*" he laughs like a fucking hyena as he thrusts his dick at me, using his hand to pretend he's holding the head of someone bobbing on his cock.

Sick.

"Buzz off, Pedro. I'm not fucking joking. Carlos already said if you caused any more trouble, he was going to evict your ass. Don't make me turn you in," I threaten.

Compared to Pedro, I'm a shrimp. I'm only five foot six and a hundred and ten pounds if I'm soaking wet. Pedro, who's fresh out of prison, has tattoos on his face for fucking crying out loud and wears wifebeaters five sizes too small. I'm no match for him in any way, shape, or form. The little knife on my key chain can barely open my mail, much less fillet the heart of a registered-sex-offender parolee.

I wrote a poem about his ass once and taped it to his door.

Pedro is built like a wall.
An ugly, graffiti, big
fucking wall.
So tall.
And solid.
But still, a big-ass wall.
If he thinks I'd ever
willingly crawl into bed
with his stinky ass,
He's got some balls.

Lark

I think he took it as some sort of advance on my part. I was just angry one night and felt like taking it out on my annoying-ass neighbor. The next morning, I blamed my moment of insanity on the vodka.

Oh, the vodka.

I only pull it out once a month on the eighteenth. The eighteenth has been the title of many poems. All of them were shredded and burned in a trash can after I cried big, ugly tears.

He holds up two fingers in a peace sign and sticks his tongue between it, licking provocatively at me. "*Te voy a hacer la sopa.*"

Enough already. "Goodbye, Pedro. Talk to me tomorrow when you're sober. And in English. Night," I groan. Then I mistakenly turn my back to him to twist the key and open my door.

The brief drop of my guard is just enough for the hardened criminal to pounce. His thick, strong arms encase me in a bear hug from behind. I can feel his erection stabbing me in the back.

"Let go!" I screech and squirm from his grasp.

He inhales my hair like a fucking lunatic. On the first, I am out of here. I don't know where I'll go, but I'm out of this hellhole. I'd rather live in box down by the river than next door to this freak any longer.

When he leans into me, my hand turns the knob on my door and we stumble inside. Shit! The last thing I need is for him to be in my place with me.

"*Te la voy a meter de mira quien viene,*" he hisses into my ear as he thrusts into my back a few times.

I'm attempting to wriggle from his grasp so I can claw his fucking eyes out when he's suddenly ripped from me.

My eyes skim right past him to the man who makes Pedro look like a twelve-year-old boy. This man is beautiful in his thunderous glory. Black hair a little on the overgrown and wild side sticks out every which direction on the top of his head, giving him a mischievous look. His eyes nearly match that of his hair, and his angry brows are furrowed as his hand closes around the throat of my punk-ass neighbor.

"Just take him next door. When he isn't high as a kite, he's not too bad. No need to kill him," I grumble.

My words seem to alert him to me, and his head snaps to look my way. Something flashes behind his eyes, and I'm incredibly curious of the man before me.

"Are you hurt?" he asks in a voice so low that I swear it rumbles right through the walls of my own chest.

Instead of answering him, I drink up his features. Strong nose. Perfect, rosy lips. Scruffy jaw.

"Let him go, Al," a growl orders from behind him.

I burst into hysterical laughter as another gorgeous man steps into my apartment beside the god of a man before me.

"What's so funny?" Al demands angrily.

Tears stream down my cheeks. Damn, I haven't laughed this hard since . . .

"Al? Really? Big, badass demigod and your name is Al?" I finally choke out past my tears.

"I'm not a *demigod,*" Al snarls as if the word is venom on his lips.

The man beside him chuckles and winks. "I'm *Omar,* and I'll take care of this guy for you."

Al's eyes remain furiously locked on mine as Omar grabs Pedro by the shirt and hauls him out of my apartment. Without my greasy neighbor between us, I fully take in the sight of him.

His olive-colored skin is flawless, and the artist within me twitches to paint that canvas. Rigid, defined muscles are encased in a tight, black T-shirt, and his jeans are dark and fitted. My eyes peruse his body without shame. When a body like this fills the entryway of your apartment, you take a moment to enjoy the beauty of it. Finally, I flit my eyes back to his, which remain fixed on my face.

"Like what you see?" he asks with a dark brow raised. One corner of his mouth twitches, and I immediately look down at the floor.

Smiles get people in trouble. Smiles cause pain.

"Something like that. Thanks for showing up on your horse, Romeo, but I'm tired as hell. Catch you later?" I steal a glance at him, and the humor is gone as he watches me.

"My brother and I are moving into the apartment across the hall from that motherfucker. We'll keep you safe," he promises.

The way his words thunder on his last line—I feel it deep down in my soul. This man is completely serious. It will be kind of nice having someone like him around to help me contend with Pedro.

"Uh, thanks, Al," I giggle.

He looks like a Dominic or a Maximus. Maybe even a Sebastian.

Something powerful and sexy. Not Al. Thoughts of Al Bundy with his hand in his pants on the show Married with Children infect my brain, and I give way to more hysterical laughter.

"Woman, are you crazy?" he asks, seeming to genuinely want to know the answer.

Yes. Certifiably so.

"Al, I'm the kind of crazy that makes insane look fun and inviting. My kind of crazy is on a whole new level."

Without warning, he stalks over to me and slides his hands into my long, thick, mahogany-colored hair. Then he tilts my head to look at him. Now that he's close, I can't help but inhale his utter masculinity. It's a scent that makes my tongue water with the desire to taste him.

"Do you ever eat?" he questions gruffly.

Hardly. When you live in a state of despair and depression, food is the last thing on your mind.

"Time to leave, Al."

His proximity is causing my heart to tense up, and I don't like the feeling. My breathing becomes shallow as I attempt to keep his smell out of my body, from infecting my very being.

When I feel his thumb stroke my jaw, my eyes flutter closed. I want to freeze this moment and live in it forever. Moments like this are rare for me. Moments where I feel free from it all.

"Promise me you'll eat more, woman."

My eyes reopen, and I smile. "Call me Lark. If you cook for me, maybe I'll eat more often."

His eyes leave mine to watch my mouth as I say my name. He seems lost in my lips. For the briefest of moments, I'd like his lips to get lost there too.

"I haven't cooked in years," he says thoughtfully. Dark eyes unwillingly leave my lips to stare deep into my green eyes.

My mouth quirks up in a half smile. "I haven't eaten in years."

His face darkens with anger—as if he knows and is pissed that I only eat ramen noodles and cereal. I can't help it though. When the mood strikes for me to eat, those are handy and easy. Although . . . my milk is usually expired and I end up whipping up ramen noodles, even for breakfast. My only vice—and truly what keeps me alive—are my Oreos. Double Stuf Oreos. Just one of my many habits . . .

"You're going to eat, baby, even if I have to spoon-feed that pretty little mouth," he flirts.

All seriousness is gone as we both break into simultaneous smiles at the idea of him feeding me.

Smiles.

Fuck.

Thump.

Chapter Three

Alpha

PALLAS WAS RIGHT. This assignment is going to be hard as shit. The black-and-white photo did nothing for the beauty that shines from Lark Miller. She hasn't told me her last name yet, but I already know so much about her from her file.

I know that she is clinically depressed and takes medication.

I know that she is estranged from her parents.

I know that she works as a tattoo artist above a bar down the street.

The file told me of her faults. Her shortcomings. Her sins. But her file failed to mention the sparkle of a sea of emeralds that twinkles in her eyes. The file never mentioned the way her smile lights up her entire face and breathes life into her soul. The fucking file never mentioned that some woman would cloud every single lesson and training I've ever received with just one look.

Just one look and I knew this FA would be the hardest damn thing I'd ever encountered.

"You're an exquisite mystery wrapped in an elegant yet razor-sharp package," I whisper as I reluctantly release her from my grip.

Her eyes flicker at my words. "A poet."

My lips are on her forehead before I can stop them, and I press a chaste kiss to her soft skin. "Words are extensions of our souls. Some people have the ability to let them out. I am one of those people, and you are worth the words."

She looks away and takes a deep breath. "Goodbye, Al the Poet." The way she says the last words is her question for my last name.

I don't even know my last name. "Just Al."

A ragged sigh. "Goodnight, Just Al."

I tear myself away from her and stalk away quickly to break free from her magnetic pull. Before I step into the hallway, I toss her a smug look.

"Be ready with that pretty little mouth open and waiting tomorrow morning," I instruct with a smirk.

Her eyes widen, and I know her mind went straight where mine did. My cock hardens at the thought of her lips all over me and—

I slip out the door and close it behind me instead of clarifying my words. The moment I'm back in the hallway, I feel a great heaviness at the loss of her company.

Lark.

My assignment.

My weakness.

"This fucking sucks," Omega grumbles from down the hallway. He's leaning up against our door with his arms folded like a damn GQ model.

"Just wait until Lovenia shows up to fuck shit up," I groan.

His eyes darken again as a smile plays at his lips. "Damn, man. Why didn't I take her to bed sooner?"

She'll be as much of a distraction to him as Lark will be to me. They spent last night and all of today together. I had to drag his naked ass out of her bed so we could catch a cab to downtown LA. He reluctantly went with me, but at least I got my partner out of there.

"Probably because she's the devil's plaything and you're a fucking angel," I laugh.

He rolls his eyes and steps away from the door so I can open it. "We're not angels. Well, not real ones yet, anyway."

I swipe the entryway light on to find an apartment identical to Lark's, only dirtier. "Well, right now, we're human, which means things are going to be that much harder. I've got your back though, dude. I still can't believe Pedro is your assignment."

Pedro was about two seconds from getting his head bashed right into Hell. Had it not been for the fact that Omega has to keep him alive for his assignment, I'd have killed him and dealt with the consequences. Lark, no matter how evil or wicked they claim she is, does not deserve to be taken advantage of by that thug.

Lark deserves better.

She's a thug too—in a different sense, but still a thug.

"Dude, I'm fucking beat," Omega whines as he stretches out on the dusty sofa that came with the apartment.

Human bodies suck. Now, we have to eat and piss and fucking sleep.

Not cool, Pallas. Not cool.

"Me too, and I have to get up early," I grumble, already feeling annoyed at my promise to feed Lark.

My duty requires me to keep her alive though, and she looks like, if she turns sideways, she'll blow off into the wind.

"Why? I'm not. Pedro is wasted, so he'll be sleeping until noon at least," he yawns.

"I need to buy some food. That girl across the hall is wasting away," I tell him as I peel my shirt off and head toward the shower.

"I've got your back, man," he calls out from the living room.

I'm going to need his back on this one.

As the shower starts, I take a deep breath. Then I step up to the sink and glance at myself in the mirror. In six years, I've done it only once before. I fucking puked all night long. It was a few weeks after I'd joined HEA, and I had already been weak to begin with. I promised myself never to look again, yet here I am, devouring the sight of myself.

"Hello, Hottie." I wink at my reflection.

There's no humor in my features. I feel lost in this human body. My stomach churns as nausea threatens to make me vomit. With shaking hands, I grab the edge of the sink and lean forward, never taking my eyes from the mirror. My bones feel brittle and achy. The human skin that covers my body begins to itch and burn. Finally, I break away from staring at those almost-black eyes of mine and stagger away from the mirror.

No answers.

Still just Al.

I'm a fucking creeper. I heard a noise in the hallway, so I'm peeking through the peephole like a Peeping fucking Tom. When I see a long mess of wavy, mahogany hair flash by, I growl and swing the door open.

"Where the hell are you going?" I demand before she makes it to the stairwell.

She freezes in her tracks. While her back is to me, I take a minute to admire her narrow waist in her long, flowing, black dress. Her arms are bare, and colorful tattoos decorate her skin. I want to see them all.

"I have places to go," she grumbles as she pulls her bag higher up her shoulder.

The drug addiction.

Fuck, I forgot all about seeing that in the file.

"I'll go with you," I assert and strut over to her.

She spins wildly to face me. Her pert nose is slightly red, as if she's been crying. Black, oversized sunglasses hide her green orbs from me.

I need to see them.

When I reach for her sunglasses, she swats me away angrily, but not before I steal them away. Bluish circles hang under her eyes like dark half-moons. The whites of her eyes are bright red. She *has* been crying.

What the fuck is her problem?

"Baby, I thought we were—"

She angrily shoves me away from her. "I am not your baby. I'll never be anyone's baby ever again!"

I'm stunned by her sudden violent behavior toward me. When I reach for her, she staggers backwards. Her eyes are wild, and she looks borderline manic.

"Let me walk you at least," I murmur.

She shakes her head and stumbles toward the stairwell. I get more nervous as hell the closer she gets to it. Fuck this. After striding over to her, I scoop her scrawny ass into my arms. Ignoring her screams and punches against my chest, I bound down the stairs as if she weighs nothing. Once at the bottom, I set her back to her feet.

"You're a big, crazy caveman lunatic!" she snarls, waving her hands franticly, both middle fingers pointed in the air.

"Cut the crap, Lark," I bellow. "I just saved your unstable ass from falling headfirst down a flight of stairs."

Her head snaps to mine and she pins me with a very serious glare. "Next time I'm about to fall to my untimely death, turn and walk the fuck away. Stay out of my life, asshole."

"Not a chance, baby. You're stuck with me for three months."

Fuck.

"Well, I'm leaving this shithole in one. See ya!" And with that, she storms out of the building and steps into the hustle and bustle of the morning commuters.

I'm barefoot but at least clothed, so I stalk after her. She's my assignment whether she likes it or not. I'll just need to tread lightly when following her. There's no way I'm letting one pretty little hair on her head get hurt on my watch.

As soon as I emerge from the building and instinctively turn my head left, I see her chocolate hair bouncing as she hauls ass down the sidewalk. Ignoring the disgusted stares at my bare feet from others, I trot after her to catch up. I stay about twenty-five feet back and slow my pace when she nears the end of the second block. When she hangs a right, her step is slower. Once I reach the corner, I peek around the side. The poor girl already lives in a shitty part of town, but she's heading right to the fucking ghetto.

The drugs.

Damn woman. Why does she have to be so difficult?

When the street is clear, she glides across the road and I send up a silent prayer that no cars come out of nowhere. I watch her come to a dilapidated building and hesitantly approach the main entrance. She scans the crowd around her, and I duck behind a telephone pole when her gaze reaches me. Once she's satisfied that nobody is after her, she slips inside.

After looking both ways, I race across the street toward the building.

"Hey, baby," a used-up whore purrs from the sidewalk. Her body is grotesquely thin, and she appears to be wearing the same dress she's been wearing for the past year. I can smell her stink from here and would bet my entire existence on the fact that she's crawling with diseases. When she smiles a toothless smile at me, I shudder.

"Ten-dollar blow job just for you, sugar," she grins and wobbles on her heels toward me.

"Not today, baby," I breathe out in a rush as I fly past her and into the building.

She mutters something about it being half off, but I ignore her and quickly take stock of my surroundings. Fuck. Lark is nowhere in sight. The entryway is dark and dirty as hell. Trash litters the floor, graffiti colors the walls, and it smells like piss.

A dark-skinned little girl appears in one of the doorways and watches me with interest as I begin making my way down the hallway and peeking in any open doors. When I reach the girl, who's no older than four, I squat down in front of her.

"Are you God?" she asks me pointedly.

I cringe at her question. It still gets me that kids seem to see right through us. We always have to be careful that they don't blow our cover. Now that I'm in human form, it is easier to hide from them, but this one still senses something unusual.

"No, doll. Not God. Have you seen a pretty girl with pictures on her skin? Brown hair almost the color of yours?" I ask.

Her tiny mouth grows into the biggest grin. "Miss Lark? Yeah. She went upstairs to the Crack Room."

Crack Room? Shit!

"Want me to show you? Momma is about to take me there. We love the Crack Room," she giggles.

Lark, what are you doing?

"No, sweetie. Stay here. I'll find it. Second floor?" I question, already striding toward the stairs.

"Right above my room." She smiles, pointing up.

I nod and bound up the stairs to take my assignment far away from this dangerous crap hole where she's influencing sweet, small children. This is worse than I thought. Pallas was right. These people are just our assignments. We shouldn't get close to them because the Reapers have a nice vacation spot for them in Hell. They are not good people like the little girl downstairs. People like Pedro and Lark need to be wiped from this Earth.

The sound of voices spills out into the hallway once I reach the second-floor landing. One of the doors on the left at the very end is open, and light pours from it into the dark hallway.

The Crack Room.

Tiptoeing, I make my way over to the room and then peek inside. What I see is so damned confusing that I have to blink several times just to make sense of it. When I finally do understand what's going on, I'm suddenly very angry.

Have I been duped?

Lark

"MISS LARK, I messed up on mine. Can I have another one?" Sha'Tanya asks. The girl is fourteen and pregnant, but when she comes to the Crack Room, she lets her inner child free.

I rip another sheet from my notebook and pass it to her.

"Anyone ready for another Oreo?" I question as I hold my bag of cookies up.

Out of the eight kids here, three raise their hands. I'm still missing little Kisha. I pass more cookies out and look toward the door. Finally though, my favorite little one bounds into the room and hugs my legs tight.

"I missed you, Miss Lark," she says sweetly with her face pressed against my legs.

"I missed you, too. Go sit down beside La'Trice and I'll bring you something to write on and some cookies.

Her mother, Corrine, smiles at me and leaves her in my care.

"Kisha, today, everyone is writing poems about something beautiful. Can you do that?" I ask as I hand her a handful of Oreos.

She nods as her dark eyes shine with delight. The little girl may not know how to write anything other than her own name right now, but she's certainly the most creative in the group. I always have them read me their poems afterwards so she doesn't get embarrassed that I can't read what hers says. She's four and the smallest of my nine "students." Sha'Tanya is the oldest and has promised to still come after she has the baby.

"I met God," she tells me knowingly with the biggest grin on her face. "And he was the prettiest man I've ever seen."

I chuckle at her words. This is the same girl who says that Santa visits her on Saturdays because she is special. And that SpongeBob eats her dinner for her when she's too full.

"Then you should write a poem about him," I smile.

She furrows her brows and sets to writing her poem. As I look around the room, my heart fills with joy. It's one of the few "highs" in life for me these days. And it's appropriate that it happens in the Crack Room. A grin tugs at my lips as I take in the view of the cracked drywall in the living room of this abandoned unit. Corrine knew the lady who used to live here and had a key. We'll use it as our own until someone kicks us out. When that happens, I'll have to come up with another place for these kids. I've been saving up in case I need to rent out a space at the rec center.

Sunday is Poem Day. These kids live for this day of the week. As long as I live, I'll never take that away from them.

An hour later on the dot, the kids all put their pencils down and look up at me expectantly. One by one, they read their sweet poems about what they find beautiful. Sha'Tanya is the second to last to read hers.

"Don't laugh or I'll beat your ass," she threatens the group.

The class giggles, and I roll my eyes.

"Don't say ass," I groan with a smile.

She smiles back and begins her poem. "My poem is called 'Beautiful Baby Boy'," she starts.

"Beautiful baby boy,
I love your toes.
Beautiful baby boy,
I love your nose.
Beautiful baby boy,
You are mine.

Beautiful baby boy,

I'll love you till the end of time."

Her eyes shine with unshed tears, and my heart does that wicked thing it does from time to time. It aches.

"Good job," I mumble and blink away my own tears.

The class claps for her, and then Kisha stands.

"My poem is called 'God is Beautiful'," she tells us proudly with a grin that could melt glaciers.

"God is beautiful.

I saw him today.

He was looking for Miss Lark.

And then he ran away.

His hair was black like my cat.

And his hair was sooooooooooo pretty.

God is beautiful.

I saw him today."

I blink in surprise at her poem. If that bastard followed me here, I'll kill—

Clap, clap, clap.

Bastard.

"So, this is what happens in the Crack Room? When do I get to do my poem?" he asks behind me.

I spin around and face the man who looks like he was dropped right out of Heaven. "Your poem?" I hiss in disgust. "You don't get to do one."

The class shrieks in shock at my sudden rudeness. That's a side they've never seen from me before.

"Why not, Miss Lark? Please," Kisha begs as she grabs my hand and tugs.

I sigh and hand him an Oreo. "Fine. Think fast."

Without missing a beat, he takes the cookie and begins his poem.

"Lark is a bad girl. So they say.

Brown hair. Green eyes. Bags under her eyes, so grey."

I glare at him.

"She thinks she has it all figured out, and maybe she does.

I can tell her right now she doesn't, because,

Things aren't always what they seem, Miss Lark.

Sometimes, an angel is found in the dark."

His poem is nonsensical bullshit. I grumble and begin gathering my pens from the kids, ignoring his smug ass. The class chatters around him, asking him questions, but I don't want to see him. He made me cry.

Well, he didn't *actually* make me cry, but he made me remember things that did. I purposefully sliced the most painful part of my life from my head and my heart. And with one innocent smile, he forced me to think about things. He forced me to climb up to the top of my closet last night, pull down that one box I have left, and touch everything in it.

I didn't sleep one wink.

I cried until my eyes burned from being so dry.

When I grab a pen and stand quickly, my world spins. Shit—ramen time. Three cookies do not constitute breakfast, it would seem. I'm going to pass out.

As soon as I begin to feel flushed and black out, strong arms hook under mine from behind and grip me tight.

"Hey there," he murmurs into my ear. "Where're you going, pretty girl?"

Pretty girl. Big liar.

I choke down the nausea in my belly and attempt to blink away some of the blackness.

We sink to the floor, and he pulls me between his spread legs with my back against his chest. The kids have dispersed and abandoned us. One hour is usually pushing it, and when that time is up, they run off to do whatever it is that kids do. Their attention can only be held for so long—hence the Oreo bribery.

"What happened?" he asks softly, his arms wrapped snuggly around my middle.

I'm so weak that I'm powerless to move against him. Instead, I try to ignore the lovely feeling of his thumb stroking my belly.

"I got dizzy."

"No shit, Sherlock. Could it be because I was right?" he whispers into my hair.

I swear he even inhales me. Sicko.

"No." My weak attempt at a fight is dusted away by his rumbling laughter, which reverberates from his chest through my back.

"Lying is a sin, you know."

God, he is so weird.

"So is breaking and entering *and* stalking. I'd say you were guilty twice now on both accounts," I argue.

The heat from his body makes me more lightheaded than before, and I can't help that I've now relaxed completely against him. My eyes feel heavy, and I just want to sleep. In his arms. Who's the sicko now?

"Okay, Lark the Lawyer. Those are not sins, baby. Those are broken laws. I could give two shits about the law. But I do care about your safety. Now, cut the crap, and let's get you some breakfast. Surely there's a diner around here."

I feel some of my strength returning, and then I notice them.

His bare feet.

There's blood on the wood floor. He's been injured.

"Why are you barefoot?" I question as I sit up to properly inspect his feet. "You're hurt."

"Some unstable woman ran off into a crowded street. What gentleman would I have been to let her run off unescorted? There was no time for shoes."

I roll my eyes and turn in his arms to look at him. Bad idea. His midnight-colored, intense eyes probe beyond the colorful surfaces of my skin. They are attempting a bold effort to peel away layers and find out what's beneath.

"I told you to leave me alone, but you don't listen," I pout.

His eyes drop to my lips, and a growl so low that it's more a vibration and less of a sound rumbles its way down to parts of my body that haven't been touched in years. "If I'd have listened, who would have caught your fall?"

I can't help but lick my lips. The way he stares at them makes me self-conscious. Do I have Oreo crumbs on them?

Another growl, this time louder.

"The floor would have caught me. We're well acquainted. I pass out a lot," I tell him like it's no big deal.

Honestly, I'm used to it. Depression, stress, grief—none of those things feed an appetite. Without an appetite, there's no desire to eat. When I don't eat, I faint. End of story. Nobody dies . . .

"No more, Lark. Do you hear me? I'll make sure you're taken care of," he assures me, his gaze still on my lips.

Another lick.

Another growl.

Don't kiss me, Al. I don't want you to kiss me.

"For three months. I remember. Glad to have you for the long haul, Just Al," I snip out sarcastically.

He brings his nose forward until it touches mine. "But I could take care of you oh so well during that time, baby."

His words are laced with insinuation, and my body reacts against my wishes. His hot, Oreo-scented breath weakens my resolve to push this man away. He's like a fucking drug. I want to smell him. Taste him. Touch him.

Too bad drugs are lame.

"You can take me to breakfast," I concede, "but that's it. Then you take me home."

He smiles. "Fine, but before we go there, I need to stop at a church and clean up my feet."

Once I nod in agreement, one of his hands unwraps from my belly and he points to the cracked mirror above the fireplace.

"That mirror makes me want to throw up."

Al is officially one fucked-up individual.

"You make me want to throw up."

I'm fucked up too.

Chapter Five

Alpha

SHE WON'T LET me carry her like I insisted upon, but she does allow me to hold her hand. It will have to do for now. The damn woman is like a walking time bomb. My work is fucking cut out for me.

"There's the church," she says softly as she raises a slender arm and points to the small building near the corner. "And there's a diner another block up."

As if we're on a Sunday stroll—well, I suppose we are—we take or time making it to the church.

"I'll wait outside on the steps," she insists.

Over my dead body.

"No. After that near fainting spell, you need to come into the air conditioning. Just sit on the pew in the back. Lie down, even. This should only take a moment," I assure her.

She groans in defeat but permits me to escort her inside. As we enter, I scan the gorgeous church to find that it appears we've arrived between services, so there are only a few people scattered about. Before I even finish surveying my surroundings, we're immediately met by Father Lester, a retired Seraph Guardian. Upon retirement, they lose their wings and once again take on a human form—the cycle a constant continuation until they meet their ultimate death and spend eternity in Heaven. I've met him on many occasions when he's come to HEA Corp for seminars or for board meetings. Since he's human now, he simply drives his old clunker downtown, no dramatic theatrics there.

"Hello, Father," I grin upon seeing him.

His eyes twinkle in surprise when he sees Lark beside me. "Hello," he greets us both with a nod.

"Can you help me in the bathroom?" I ask as I guide Lark to a pew like I promised.

She sits down and buries her face in her knees.

Father Lester's gaze flickers to her once again, and then he turns on his heel. I follow him down the back hallway, through a set of double doors, and into his office. After he shuts the door behind him, he looks up at me questioningly.

"Who's the girl?" he asks.

"Lark Miller. My final assignment."

He waves his hand toward his personal bathroom—the one I know won't have a mirror.

"What happened to your feet?"

I groan. "My subject is accident-prone. I had to run after her. There was no time for shoes. She's safe now."

He nods, and I make my way into the bathroom. After I've washed and dried my feet, I walk back into his office. Then he pulls a pair of shoes from the closet.

"We keep things on hand for the homeless. You're in luck," he says with a smile.

In the short time since I've been here, I've felt my strength growing. "Thanks, Father Lester."

His eyes scrutinize me. "Lark is pretty. Don't become attached, Alpha."

I nod immediately. I know the rules well. "Of course not, Father. Just keeping her safe."

He purses his lips into a fine line before saying his last piece. "If the temptations of that woman become too strong, come see me. The SG want you, and you deserve to be a part of the elite. I've seen your files, son. I know how hard FA is—trust me. It nearly killed me, but I remembered who I wanted to be, not who I was before. Keep your eye on the prize. Those wings will be yours."

I absently listen to him drone on, but all I keep replaying in my head are the words, "*It nearly killed me, but I remembered who I wanted to be, not who I was before.*"

He remembered who he was before?

"Bless you, son," he says in conclusion and places his hand on my shoulder.

The last of my depleted energy is restored. Coming here was smart.

"Thank you, Father. I'll stay focused." I hate the way my voice quivers.

I *hope* I can stay focused.

"I'll have some scrambled eggs," Lark tells the waitress with hair so red that it's almost pink.

The waitress raises a brow that suspiciously matches her hair at Lark. "That's it?" Then she pops her gum her.

"Yep," Lark snaps.

The two women hold each other's glares before the waitress finally looks up at me. Her smile is bright, and she bats her eyelashes. "Hey there, handsome. What can I get you besides a side of Red?"

When she winks at me, Lark actually growls like a little puppy. It's cute as hell.

"I'll have the big stack of pancakes with extra butter. Four eggs over medium. Hash browns—extra crispy. Double bacon and sausage. And," I say as I peruse the menu one last time, "a yogurt parfait. I have to watch my figure." I wink back at her.

The waitress blushes. "Your figure is pretty perfect, but a man needs to eat." Then she bounces off to fill our order.

My eyes follow her away for a moment as I wonder how in the heck someone gets their fake eyebrows to match their fake hair.

"You're a pig," Lark spits out in disgust.

I snap my attention to her and really take her in. Her dark hair hangs wildly in front of her shoulders. With the sun shining in the window, every hair holds a different shade of brown. I think I even see a few strands of gold. Green eyes flicker with anger as she glares at me.

Pink lips form an annoyed pout, and I have to look anywhere besides those lips if I have any hope of keeping my job.

"I'm hungry. I haven't eaten in ages." That's the damn truth. Besides that Oreo, I haven't put one morsel of food in my mouth in six long years. Eating might be a pain in the ass, but food is pretty fucking good, so it makes up for the annoyance.

"Not your appetite, nerd. You're a pig. A man-whore. I saw the way you watched her walk away. Was her ass cute? Her face sure as hell wasn't." Her brow is raised disdainfully as she meets my shocked stare.

Is she fucking kidding me right now?

"I was not checking out her ass," I scoff. "Trust me. I'm not interested in the women around here."

Her eyes dart away from me, and she frowns, appearing to be stung by my comment.

"Drink your orange juice," I order.

The hurt is gone as her gaze meets mine again. She's angry. I can't win with this woman.

Thankfully, she appeases me and picks her glass up. Slowly, she sips the juice. After several moments, she begins to regain some of her color. I see a smile play at her lips.

"What's so funny, baby?" I question with one eyebrow cocked in question and a smirk of my own.

"You're so bossy. And I hate to be bossed around. Yet, somehow, here we are, having breakfast together. God's mysterious ways," she chuckles and downs more of her juice.

I bristle at her comment. If she only knew.

"Tell me about yourself, Lark," I insist in an effort to change the subject. "Clearly, there's more than meets the eye with you."

Her file says a lot about her that I just haven't found to be true. There's so much about her that isn't in that file. I'd like to draw my own conclusions.

"More than meets the eye? I'm a twenty-seven-year-old loser who works at a crummy tattoo shop. My family hates me. I hate them. And I have depression, not an eating disorder. End of story."

I stare at the enigma in front of me. She may think she's good at steeling her emotions, but I can see right through them. This sharp-tongued woman before me is hurting. There's a hole in her heart as big as fucking Texas.

"Hate is a strong word," I say softly.

She laughs bitterly. "Well, when you need someone—when your life takes a nosedive into the darkest fucking territory you've ever encountered—you expect your family to be by your side. You expect them to understand, not to tell you, 'It's time to move on.' I'll never move on."

Move on from what? Her file never spoke of anything traumatic.

"Care to elaborate?" I ask.

Her eyes fly to mine and she furrows her brows in such a hateful manner that it effectively knocks the breath out of me. "No, I do not care to elaborate."

A pop of gum alerts me that our waitress has arrived with our food, interrupting the tense moment.

"I brought you extra syrup, sugar. You look like you could use a little extra sweetness in your life." She smiles at me and then glances contemptuously over at Lark.

Lark rolls her eyes as if the woman's blatant rudeness doesn't bother her in the least. Once she leaves us with all of our food, I watch Lark as she pokes at her eggs with a fork.

"You will eat all of that, woman," I instruct in a soft yet firm tone.

Her green eyes lazily find mine, and there's a hollowness behind them. A simple nod is what she offers, but once again, I see through her eyes.

"You will eat those eggs or I'll embarrass the shit out of you and feed you like a child," I threaten.

This time, she glares at me and shoves a huge forkful of eggs in her mouth. With her mouth open, she chomps exaggeratedly. Unfortunately for her, I'm a guy. Chewing with her mouth open won't gross me out. I all but inhale my food, but my eyes never leave her. I'll make sure she eats every last bite.

"Done. Are you happy?" she asks in annoyance after she swallows the last of her eggs.

I push the untouched yogurt parfait toward her. "Nope. Eat this too."

"Are you kidding me right now?"

I raise an eyebrow, but my face remains serious. "Do I look like I'm kidding right now?"

An exasperated sigh bursts from her before she picks the spoon up and begins to slowly eat the parfait. Finally, she sets the spoon down and looks at me.

"Why do you care if I eat or not? Why do you suddenly feel the need to insert yourself into my life? We're neighbors. Not friends. Not boyfriend and girlfriend. Not anything. And we won't ever be. Lark Miller doesn't make friends. Lark Miller doesn't date. Lark Miller just floats through life until death steals her away. And for the safety of others, I hope that happens soon," she says wistfully.

I grimace at her words. Three long fucking months. The girl is practically ready to slit her wrists here at the table. How in the hell am I going to keep her alive for three months?

"You're mine for three months, Lark. Then you can go on your merry little way," I grumble.

Her eyes fill with tears, and the confusion is evident on her features.

All I need is three months. She will get her warm vacation away from this place she hates so much and then I'll get my wings.

We're all winners.

Chapter Six

Lark

GO AWAY, AL.

God, will he ever leave me the hell alone? I'm sitting on my countertop in my kitchen as he slams cabinet doors.

"Where the fuck is all of your food?" he demands angrily.

I shrug my shoulders. "At the store beside the ramen noodles and Oreos."

He scowls at me. "Don't be a smartass."

He's pissed, which causes a smile to tug at my lips. For some reason, I'm learning that one of those "highs" in life is pissing Just Al off. I love the way his dark eyebrows bunch together and make him look like an angry cartoon. His normal easygoing demeanor is replaced by a fierce glint. I like pushing this button of his.

"I don't have any food. God, will you just go back to your apartment already? I want to sleep before I have my shift," I groan.

He stalks toward me and pushes my knees apart so he can stand close. The sudden intimate movement causes my heart to flop in my chest. My heart doesn't flop. My heart doesn't do anything.

"Leave," I snarl and point toward the door.

His furious, black eyes dart back and forth as he studies me. Instead of moving away, he slides his hands up the outside of my thighs and rests them on my hips. My breath pauses in my throat.

"Why do I piss you off so badly, Lark?"

I tear my eyes from his and look down at my hand. As if he understands, he slides his big, warm hand over my left one. A wicked tear escapes and splashes the top of his.

"You have three months to tell me, baby."

Another splash.

I gasp when he raises his other hand and swipes my cheek dry. This man in front of me ruins everything. He messes up my carefully constructed world that protects the most vulnerable piece of me—my heart. I hate that he thinks he can waltz in here and practice his voodoo magic on me. The part of me that usually stays under lock and key rattles behind its door in his presence.

"Just go, Just Al."

His fingers find my hair, tangling them into the wild mess, and tilts my head back up. The anger is gone, and compassion pours from those liquid-coal eyes. I hate the way he attempts to see inside me. Nobody is allowed there ever again.

"I'll figure you out eventually," he promises. With another chaste kiss to my forehead, he tears away from me.

The moment the apartment door slams, I burst into tears. I sure hope he doesn't ever figure me out.

After hopping off the counter, I shakily make my way to my bedroom. My steps are slow and agonizing. Half of me begs me not to do it. The other pleads for me to go faster.

I need it like I need to breathe.

For so long, I denied its pull. I didn't need to bury myself in the scents of the past. It's been years since I've even opened that box.

Don't do it, Lark.

I ignore the logical side of my brain. The craving is too strong now. After last night, just one touch of that box and I was addicted once again. The same box that pushed the final wedge between my parents and me calls out to me.

When I reach my closet, I push my ottoman inside and step onto it. The box isn't any bigger than twelve inches by twelve inches, but my world exists inside.

"I missed you," I say in a whispered breath as I pull down the box.

After stepping off the ottoman with it, I walk over to my bed and sit down. When I open it, the smells of my past assault me. Ignoring the pictures, I pull out the T-shirt I used to sleep in every single night. One night, though, I stopped sleeping in it and stored it in this box instead. I chose to preserve it.

My eyes flit over to the clock on my nightstand. Seven hours until my shift. I know this is a mistake, but I'm greedy today. Today, I need this one simple comfort. Carefully, I bring the shirt to my nose.

Please, God.

Tears roll from my eyes and wet the fabric as I inhale it. Then I collapse onto my pillows and bury my face in the shirt. If I close my eyes, I can pretend. I'll allow myself this one luxury.

Black eyes instead of blue.

Just Al fills my thoughts, and I sob hysterically. This is why I don't use that fucking wretched, useless organ. I loathe the part of my body that pumps blood to my extremities. I hate the part of me that aches suddenly after it was lying dormant for quite some time. It isn't fair. Just Al isn't supposed to make me feel.

Just Al is the devil.

I'm fucking late. Again.

I'm honestly not quite sure why they haven't fired me yet, but then I remember. They know I'm a diamond in the rough. My art is beautiful and I'm cheap.

Sighing, I twist my long, dark hair into a messy bun. There's no time for makeup, so I skip it and begin wrenching drawers open, looking for something to wear to work.

My eyes roam over to the clock again. Ten after seven. Fuck!

I settle on a loose, black tank top and a pair of cut-off, denim shorts. Once I've yanked my dress off, I unhook my bra and toss it to the floor. When I dive into my art, I can't be fucking confined. Then I slip on my tank and pull my shorts up over my black panties. From across the room, I spy my combat boots, so I grab a pair of ankle socks and stride over to them. Once completely dressed, I walk over to the mirror and look at my reflection. My tattoos color my skin and mark my journey through this bullshit life. Some I wish were gone. Others I couldn't live without.

I look like a fucking joke.

Good.

When I lean forward to tie my boots, my cleavage hangs out and I see the six tattooed stars between my breasts. My favorites. All six of them.

Six.

Beautiful.

Stars.

I snatch my huge, black bag from my dresser and storm from my bedroom. Lunch and dinner are no-gos today as I bolt out the front door. I'm already late and don't have time for much more. With an annoyed sigh, I turn to lock my door and hear footsteps coming toward me.

Fucking Pedro.

But when I whir around, my keys bared as a weapon, I hate the feeling of relief that floods me when I see the onyx eyes of Al.

"I made dinner," he says and hands me a fucking Hot Pocket.

"Wow," I say sarcastically as I take the food from him. "You really went all out."

He grins his stupidly alluring lopsided grin. "A man has to cook for his woman."

God, I hate him.

"I'm late," I groan as I walk past him. Then I nibble the food I'm secretly thankful for.

"I'll walk you."

Just Al is just so fucking annoying.

"Fine. Suit yourself. A hot little piece of meat like yourself will get hounded by every damn streetwalker along the way. Consider yourself warned," I smart off as I bound toward the stairs.

Tonight, I am hungry, so I quickly devour the Hot Pocket. As I begin descending the stairs, Al loops his arm in mine and matches my pace as he escorts me. At the bottom, he releases me, and then we walk in silence toward the tattoo shop. It's five blocks up, and by the time we have hoofed it over there, I've already burned through the energy from the food he gave me. When we step in front of the building, I wave goodbye to him and stomp up the stairs to the second floor above the bar.

"You're late," Gus grumbles as I burst through the front doors.

"Sorry," I mutter, making a beeline straight for my station.

"You've been booked for the entire night. Big tattoo appointment," he calls out after me.

Another pussy biker? Unfuckingbelievable.

I ignore his statement and begin prepping my tools. After fifteen minutes, I feel the presence of someone standing behind me. When I turn to greet my customer and see who it is, I frown.

Just fucking Al.

"You have to be kidding me," I hiss and throw my hands up in the air in disbelief.

His eyes flicker, and I sense brief apprehension.

"Fine. How many tattoos do you have, Al?"

With hooded eyes, he blinks sheepishly at me. A blank canvas? The inner artist in me rubs her palms together in anticipation.

"None? Okay, Just Al. You've piqued my interest," I admit. "What do you want?"

He flicks his eyes to the door and stalks over to me. I ignore how nice he looks in his tight, white T-shirt and fitted jeans. My eyes refuse to peek at his hair—the hair that seems hell-bent on begging me to mess it the fuck up with my fingers.

"I'm embarrassed," he murmurs.

Now I am completely intrigued. The bossy man I spent the morning with is suddenly acting shy around me.

"Spill, Al."

He groans but peels his shirt off. Peels the protection off. Peels off that one piece that separates me from his blank, untouched skin.

My eyes greedily devour every unflawed inch of it. Every contour of his chest is analyzed and catalogued by my eyes.

"Where?"

"My back."

He turns and reveals even more perfection. Untouched skin. Tan but perfect. Not a birthmark or freckle. No moles. No scars. No hair.

The room spins even though I filled my little belly.

"Straddle the chair," I instruct.

He doesn't hesitate before he tosses one leg over the side of the seat. Once he sits, his hard ass pokes out.

"What do you want?" I question. I can't imagine what a tattoo virgin would want that would take up my entire night. There's no way he can sit here for hours as I mark him. No fucking way.

"Lark?" He turns his head to look at me. Something dark flashes his features, and I get a sick feeling in my stomach.

"What, Al?"

"I want wings. That's all I've ever wanted."

I swallow down the emotion in my throat. Wings. Everyone wants fucking wings.

"What kind of bird?" I ask as I begin prepping my gun.

Silence.

Finally, I glance over my shoulder at him.

Sadness.

Why is he so sad?

"Not a bird. Angel wings."

I bite my lip. Of course. Just Al *would* want fucking angel wings.

Chapter Seven

Alpha

I CAN'T BELIEVE I'm doing this. Pallas warned me that what I do while on this FA would be permanent. Do I want to live my entire existence with tattooed angel wings on my back? Wings that would eventually hide under the real ones I'll be awarded once I become one of the elite?

"Make them beautiful, Lark." My only request.

She doesn't respond. Instead, I hear her tinker with her tools. I smother my face in the vinyl of the bed I'm straddling. Her smell suffocates me. The sweet scent of her shampoo. A faint scent of deodorant. A hint of pizza sauce from the Hot Pocket earlier.

What am I doing?

You're watching your assignment . . .

Am I?

Skinny little legs climb on top of me. She can't weigh more than a gust of wind, I think to myself as I feel her settle with her legs spread and her ass on mine. My dick thickens painfully beneath me—it certainly likes her there.

"Tell me about what you want, Just Al."

Just Al.

"You're the artist. I'll love whatever you create."

That's the truth. Somehow, I trust my words.

"Wow. You don't know me at all. Yet somehow, you're willing to let me have creative reign. Are you sure about that, big boy?"

Big boy. Not Al. Or Just fucking Al. *Big boy.* My cock is painfully pressing against the bed.

"I trust you. Don't break my trust."

She doesn't agree or disagree before she begins her painful artwork. The first pinch is the worst, but soon, I'm able to dull it away by losing myself to the recesses of my mind. Then I close my eyes and disappear.

"Please quit."

"It's not that easy."

"What if you don't come back?"

"I will come back."

"All done, Just Al," Lark whispers as she wipes my back with something wet.

How long have I been lost in my head?

I suppress a groan when she climbs off me, and with it, she takes her heat. I'm almost tempted to have her tattoo my chest so she can straddle me for several more hours.

"It looks okay," she lies.

Our first meeting may have just been last night, but I can read her easily already. Right now, the slightly playful tone in her voice tells me that she's lying. In this instance, I'm glad.

"Lying is a sin," I remind her with a smile. Then I climb off the bed and stretch my legs.

As I adjust to standing after hours on the chair, I scan her face as she regards me. The bags under her eyes are darker than they were last night. She's tired.

"Come on. Let's get you home," I tell her firmly.

Hurt flashes across her features before she finally steels her face into a hard look. "The mirror is over there."

I squash a groan in my throat and walk over to it. Turning my back to it, I glance over at her. The expression on her face is hopeful. She wants me to love this tattoo. When her green eyes meet mine, I wink at her and smile, assuring her that I'll like it.

Peering over my shoulder, I finally get a glimpse. I feel like puking—not from the art but from the damn reflection. The wings in their delicate and detailed beauty are more than I could ever have imagined. I don't like them at all.

I fucking love them.

The mirror has its wicked ways with me, and then I stumble away from it, toward the widening eyes of Lark.

"I'm going to be sick," I grunt and burst past her.

The room is a blur all the way into the bathroom, where I lose the three Hot Pockets I ate before Lark came out of her apartment. Mirrors are the devil.

Once I'm sure I've emptied my stomach, I rush over to the sink and rinse my mouth, careful to avoid my reflection. I won't be able to see the wings often, but I'll always know they are there. Somehow, the art she just permanently painted on my back gives me strength.

Lark gave me my wings.

When I emerge from the bathroom, I see her cleaning her tools, her back to me. Her ass is cute in her short, denim shorts, and my dick hardens again as I think about how she was straddling me for hours.

Too bad we weren't in her bed for that.

My thoughts seize me and guilt consumes me. Lark is a temptation, and I can't succumb to her. She's my job.

She drops a piece of metal she was messing with and it clatters to the floor. Spinning to face me, she bends over to retrieve it.

Six.

Beautiful.

Stars.

Her full breasts should be the focal point right about now. I should, because I'm a fucking man, be focusing on the erect, pink nipples that stand up on full display as her chest is fully bared to me. But I can't take my eyes off her tattoos.

A pain slices me so deep in my chest that I nearly collapse. That mirror will be the death of me. Although, a part of me knows it isn't residual effects from the mirror—it's entirely something else.

Green eyes fly to mine and discover that they're glued to her chest. With a quick swoop, she picks the metal up and stands. Once she's no longer revealing her pert tits to me, the room stops spinning.

"Peep shows are extra, Al." She smirks and then turns her back to me.

My eyes skitter across every colored piece of her bare skin that is exposed to me. This woman is too much.

"Here, you need to let me protect your tattoo." With a little twirl of her finger, she motions for me to turn around. As I do as I'm told, I hear her tear a piece of plastic wrap from a roll and gently spread it across my back. Her fingertips skitter over my skin as she uses pieces of tape to hold it in place. The way she touches my flesh, so delicately and carefully, makes me wonder how it would feel for her to touch me everywhere. I bet it would feel like Heaven.

"All done, big boy."

Pushing those treacherous thoughts from my head, I grab my shirt and carefully pull it on over my body. "Hurry up. I'll walk you home."

As we walk arm in arm up the stairs to our floor, I sense that something is off and I'm immediately on guard. Loud music is blasting from an open door—Pedro's open door.

"Stay behind me," I order, and thankfully, she listens.

Slowly, I tiptoe over to the door and peek inside. What I see makes my heart sink, but I know he's only doing his job. Pedro is lying back, smoking a joint while he hungrily watches the scene in front of him. Omega is on the couch with his legs spread apart. None other than Lovenia is straddling him and teasing him with kisses. His hands are firmly planted on her barely-covered-by-her-tight-dress ass.

The Leviathan is here to fuck shit up. As if shit isn't already hard enough. I hope to God this is all part of Omega's game—to become buddies with his assignment to keep an eye on him.

A lust-filled moan escapes Lovenia, and Pedro sits up with his elbows on his knees. Omega urges the scantily clad Lovenia to ride his cock harder. The sounds coming from both of them hardly seem like an act. Omega needs to keep his head on straight around that woman.

I turn toward Lark and take hold of her hand. "Come on," I whisper and hurry her past the open door, toward her apartment.

"Can I come inside?" I ask as she begins pulling her keys out.

Her green eyes find mine and she searches for something. For what, I don't know.

"For a minute, and then go home," she finally concedes as she unlocks and pushes her door open. She dumps her purse on the entryway table and then makes a beeline for the kitchen. "Want a drink?" Her question comes from the other room.

Even though I've been here a couple of times, I've never took the time to look around. My eyes take the time to inspect her space. Ratty-ass couch. Crummy furniture. No pictures on the wall. No décor. Nothing. Who is Lark Miller?

"Sure," I answer absentmindedly as I lock the door behind me.

"Good. I didn't really want to drink alone," she calls out.

I tear my gaze from the living room and stalk over to the kitchen. Her cute ass wiggles as she reaches as high as she can from her knees on the countertop for something on the top shelf of the cabinet. The baggy, black shirt she's wearing rides up and I see a flash of the colored skin on her back. My fingers twitch to touch her there.

Lark is a temptation. She is a job.

Finally, her hands find purchase on what she was looking for. She pulls a giant bottle of vodka down and hands it to me. Then she snags a shot glass before scrambling out of the cabinet and sitting her ass on my now favorite piece of kitchen counter real estate. Oh, to be that countertop . . .

"I normally save this for the eighteenth of every month, but today calls for a special occasion," she practically spits out.

The eighteenth. Noted. Fourteen days away.

She extends a long, slender hand toward me, and for a moment, I'm tempted to turn it over and kiss the top of it. But I quickly realize she wants the liquor. Dumbly, I hand it to her and watch her make quick work of unscrewing the cap and filling the glass.

"Cheers to fucking nothing," she laughs bitterly before downing the vodka.

I don't understand her sudden mood change, but it unnerves me. She fills the glass again, yet now, she hands it to me. Then her green eyes find mine and a flash of hate flickers in them. I don't like the look at all and am confused by it.

"What's wrong, Lark?" I ask with the glass poised at my lips.

Emerald eyes glisten but then fall to my lips at the glass. This time, they shine with an emotion I like. An emotion that has my cock once again thickening in my jeans.

"What's right, Al?"

An enigma wrapped in a puzzle box. Her words always have double meanings, and I intend to find out what she means.

I toss the shot back and hand the glass to her. The vodka burns a trail down my throat right into my belly. I shouldn't be drinking while on the job, but it's keeping me here with her, so I do it anyway.

"Al, I did a good job."

I'm puzzled by her words.

She gulps down another shot and points a quivering finger at me. "Take off your shirt."

Frowning at her, I shake my head. "I'm not going to have sex with you, Lark."

Her eyes widen in shock before she quickly pins me with a nasty glare. "I don't have sex with people named Al. Now take off your shirt and let me see your back, asshole."

Oh.

Shit.

I meet her furious gaze and, without hesitation, peel my T-shirt from my body. Her eyes briefly fall to my chest before she motions for me to turn around.

"I did a good job," she whispers again.

When her delicate fingers dust across my skin, I wince. Her touch is like fire on my raw skin. And even though it hurts like a bitch, I don't want her to stop.

She's my temptation.

My dick agrees and leaps to life.

Then her hand suddenly pulls away from me. I look over my shoulder to see if she's done admiring her handiwork and see her removing her top.

Fuck.

I spin around so fast that I nearly topple over. With her tank gone, her long, dark hair hangs in front of her luscious tits. They're fucking amazing, and I've seen a lot of tits.

"Lark." All I can manage to stammer out is her goddamned name.

One of her mahogany eyebrows rises as she meets my gaze. My eyes are snared in this bullshit trap she's pulling.

"Touch me, Just Al."

Someone growls like a fierce lion, and I'm about to clobber said person until I realize that it was me. The possessive, hungry animalistic sound that echoed in the small kitchen belonged to me. Exhaling with a sharp breath, I step forward and tentatively cup one of her breasts. My thumb grazes across her nipple.

"More," she begs in a quiet voice.

I press my dick against the counter and give her nipple a pinch. With my other hand, I snake it around her waist and pull her to me. She smells like fucking heaven.

I dip my head down against her neck until my lips connect with her skin. Her long, thin fingers slide into my hair and she grips me tight. With a dart of my tongue, I sample her flesh. When I suck her into my mouth, she moans so loudly—and with so much want—that I nearly push her back and fuck her into oblivion.

Once I start with this woman, I'll never be able to stop.

"Why don't you like my wings?" she murmurs, out of the blue.

Her question confuses me, and I unwillingly tear my lips from her skin so that I can look at her. Our noses are so close, and my thumb doesn't stop its reverent rubbing across her nipple.

"Wings?" I question. She doesn't have wings.

"Al, you're wacky. I'm talking about the tattoo." Hurt once again morphs her features.

"Lark, it's amazing. Those wings are beautiful, just like I knew they would be."

She blinks away a tear. "Then why did you throw up? Why have you not mentioned one word about it?"

Does Lark Miller really care what I think?

"I hate mirrors, but the glimpse that I did see was perfect." I grin and look deep into her eyes.

She smiles back and flutters her eyes closed when my fingers skitter between her breasts to skim over the tattoos there.

"You're a star, Lar," I tell her playfully.

Her hand comes out of nowhere and slaps me so hard on my cheek that I wonder if I'll bruise.

"Get out of my apartment!" she screams before pushing me forcefully away from her.

I stumble back and look at the wild woman before me. She's losing her marbles right in front of me. When I don't move, she slings the shot glass at me, and it hits me in the chest.

"What the hell, woman?" I roar back, my chest now smarting in pain.

Her green eyes are liquid crazy. She picks up the vodka bottle and lobs it with all her might in my direction. This I do dodge, but I still get soaked by the liquor. My back screams in pain when some dribbles down, but I don't move.

"Please leave," she sobs, her anger quickly subsiding.

I don't know what's going on with her, but I sure as shit am not leaving her now.

She slides off the cabinet and stumbles forward. Lightning quick, I envelop her in my arms. Then I brace myself for her to scratch me, bite me, or beat the shit out of me. Instead, she presses her soft breasts against my wet, bare chest and cries.

And cries.

Several minutes in of holding her up while she loses herself to hysterics, I wonder what is really going on with her. Her file claims that she's awful. My experience with her tells me that she's sad.

"Come on, baby. I'm putting you in bed," I murmur into her hair before scooping her into my arms.

Her tears have become sniffles and hiccups. Talking long strides, I make my way into her bedroom. I sit her on the edge of the bed and grab an old T-shirt that sits on the comforter. With no complaint, she lets me push it over her head, and I help her arms through the holes.

"Stand up," I instruct.

Shakily, she does as she was told, and I fumble with the button on her jean shorts. Eventually, my wobbly fingers manage to get the zipper down. I don't know if the quivering in my hands is from the alcohol or the niggling worry that has seeped into my bones, but either way, I don't feel so hot. Sliding my thumbs into the tops, I push them down but leave her panties on. The shorts drop to her ankles, and she steps out of them.

I pull the covers on her bed back and help her in. While she gets settled, I move a box from her bed over to her dresser and kick my shoes off.

"What are you doing?" She wants to be combative, I can tell, but the fight in her is gone.

"I'm taking care of you, just like I promised."

A big sigh comes from the bed as she rolls over onto her side. I take my jeans off before climbing into the bed beside her. Once settled next to her, I haul her warm body into the curve of mine.

More sobs.

My body feels beat and I need to rest. But I need to make sure she's okay. I stroke her belly through her T-shirt in what I hope is a soothing manner. My mind briefly envisions this woman nestled into me, wearing a simple, white gown and a sheer veil that hides her perfection from me.

Minders don't get married.

Seraph Guardians don't get married.

Assignments destined for Hell don't get married.

So push the goddamned beautiful vision right from your head, Alpha.

Chapter Eight

Lark

SOMETIMES, WORDS CAN hurt worse than any physical infliction. Sometimes, words can be a reminder—a painful one at that. And sometimes, words can rip the scab off a god-awful wound that won't stop fucking bleeding.

Words suck.

As day seeps into my bedroom, I'm awoken with a blasting headache and the heat of someone suffocating me.

"I sleep alone."

"You don't now."

"You're impossible."

"You love me."

Grabbing hold of the heavy arm, I heave it away from me. Soft snores stop as I sit up in bed. My gaze drifts down to the T-shirt I'm wearing, and I gasp in horror. I'd hoped it was a dream. It was not.

With a huff, I yank the shirt off and fold it with an obsessive neatness that I've perfected over the years. Ignoring the stare from the one on my bed, I pad over to the box and slide the shirt in. I don't care that my body is nearly naked in front of him. I don't care that he sees me trying in a desperate attempt to hide my past. His eyes follow me from the dresser with my box to my closet. I'm climbing up onto the ottoman to put the box away when I hear the springs of my bed. A cringe shudders through me when I hear heavy footsteps approach me.

The box nearly crashes to the floor when hot hands grasp my hips to hold me steady. This fucking man is so goddamned obsessed with my safety. I huff as I push the box onto the shelf.

"I'm not a china doll," I grumble and turn in his grip.

His perfect hair is a mess, and he looks so delicious. The taut muscles in his chest are worthy of my tongue, and I lick my lips. Black eyes study me with an expression I don't comprehend, but for some reason, I like it.

As I step off the ottoman, he refuses to let me go. I get lost in his scent and glance down to escape his hungry gaze. Big mistake. His thick cock is standing proudly in its morning glory, straining to rip through the black fabric of his boxers.

I want to touch it.

I hate myself.

Wrenching away, I stalk toward the bathroom. He follows me but doesn't go into the bathroom with me—just remains outside the door.

"Go home, Al."

He doesn't respond as I shed my panties and turn the shower on. Wondering if he's watching, my eyes flit over to the doorway, where he is looking every bit a Greek god with his sculpted body and otherworldly sexiness. His arms are folded across his chest, and he's leaning on the side of his shoulder in the doorjamb, watching me, his coal eyes following my every move. A thrill courses through me, and I instantly reject it.

"Lark," he growls, "tell me about you. I need to know about the real you."

I am the *me* I always was. I am the *me* who didn't exist for a short time all those years ago. This is the only *me* he'll get.

"I hate people. There. You know me," I smart off as I climb into the not-quite-hot spray of the shower.

He grumbles something in response, but I can't hear him over the shower. Instead, I begin shampooing my hair. But then the curtain rips open and his black eyes skim my naked body before flashing up to meet my gaze.

"Meet me at my apartment in an hour. I'll make breakfast."

Damn him and his bossy ways.

"Fine. Now either get in or get out," I snap.

After an exaggerated pause, he closes the curtain and gets out.

I ignore the disappointment.

I chew on my lip as I stand in front of his apartment with my hand poised to knock. Something keeps me from actually making the sound though. But when I hear Pedro's door open, I rap on the door with urgency.

"You must be Lark," a sultry voice purrs from behind me.

I spin around to see the beautiful woman from the night before. The woman who was riding Omar like a bull while Pedro watched. When I realize she came from his apartment without Omar in tow, I know she's a ho.

"Yep," I clip out.

I'm saved from her friendliness when the door swings open. Omar flashes me a smile, but once he sees the woman, his brown eyes darken.

Sorry, buddy. She slept with the disease fest across the hallway.

"Lovenia, have you met Lark?" he asks, his eyes still trained on her.

She slides her hand up my shoulder and swipes my still-damp hair out of the way. "We just met. *Om—*"

"*Omar,* can you go check on my bacon?" Al asks, interrupting her, and then gives them each a pointed look.

I turn to look at Lovenia once more, and understanding passes over her features. The way they all spoke without speaking pisses me right the fuck off. I would leave them to their little threesome, but the smell of bacon has already lured me in.

Al steps out into the threshold and takes my hand. "Come on, Twiggy."

Twiggy?

Lovenia giggles and scoots past us into the apartment. Her tight, red dress hugs her luscious curves, which makes me jealous. I feel like a little girl compared to this woman. Why I care, I don't know. But when Al's dark eyes stay trained on *mine* and his warm hand squeezes *mine,* I feel a small victory.

"If you want me to keep this breakfast date of ours, I suggest you don't call me that again," I warn.

He chuckles and dips down to plant a kiss on my forehead. "I'll call you Twiggy until you stop being a twig," he smirks. "Now come inside and let me fatten you up."

I sigh in frustration but let him lead me into the apartment. Omar has Lovenia pressed against the refrigerator and is kissing the hell out of her. She makes me sick. He seems like a nice enough guy—clearly doesn't deserve someone who would sleep with Pedro. Pedro is the bottom-of-the-barrel pond scum.

That makes Lovenia a bottom feeder.

"Plates are in that cabinet next to the lovebirds," Al tells me as he tends to the food on the stove.

I ignore the slurping of the couple that is every bit magazine-cover worthy and pull out four plates. After I set the plates next to the stove, Al turns it off and faces me.

"You look nice today, Lark."

His simple compliment warms me, but I don't let it show.

"Looks can be deceiving," I wink.

He rolls his eyes and begins dishing up food. "Extra eggs for Twiggy."

I snatch my plate and stalk over to the table. The lovebirds have broken apart and are playing grab-ass now while they fill their plates. Al moves around the kitchen as if he'd been born to be there. At seeing him as he effortlessly steps around the two horsing around and pours glasses of orange juice, something tugs at my heart.

He's so content. Happy, even. I envy his ease at life. Some of us struggle to be normal enough to eat eggs.

When he saunters over carrying our juice, I grill him.

"So, what do you do for work? You act like following me is your job," I mouth off. Then I shove a bite of eggs into my mouth.

His eyes widen, and a utensil that Omar drops clatters in the kitchen behind him. "I work—"

Lovenia finishes for him. "They work for the government. It's classified, sweetie."

I hate his woman. Al nods, but I don't believe any of them. It's all bullshit. The three of them are bizarre as hell.

"And I'm the Queen of Fucking England. It's okay. I thought we were becoming friends, *Just Al.* Looks like we're *just acquaintances,*" I tell him snootily before I shovel more eggs in.

"Oh, sweetie, I'd say by the way he watches you, he'd love to be more than *just friends.* I bet you fuck like an animal," Lovenia says.

"That's enough, Lovenia," Al growls.

She has the sense to look embarrassed and innocently bats her eyelashes at him. "Just playing Cupid, *Al.*"

I scoff at her words. "Save your arrows, Cupid. I don't fall in love. You'd have to have a heart left for that."

Her brows fly to her hairline, but then she schools her features. "I'm making you two my special project. I would be willing to bet Al's top-secret job on my ability that I'll get that heart of yours beating again for that hunk over there. You can thank me later."

"Lovenia," Omar and Al warn in unison.

She smiles sweetly once again, but I am onto her game.

"Can you pass the salt please?" she asks me as if we didn't just have the weirdest conversation.

I take a deep breath and pass it to her.

Who are these people and why are they suddenly in my life?

Chapter Nine

Alpha

I CAN MAKE it two and a half more months.

The first couple of days were rough, but Lark and I have fallen into something that works for us. Each day, she comes over for breakfast. I take her out to lunch. And then, on nights she works, we have a walking dinner. Even though it's been two weeks of this routine, she remains tightlipped about her past, but at least she hasn't had any more breakdowns. She and Lovenia keep their claws bared when around each other, but thus far, no blood has been drawn.

"Mustard," Lark barks, wrenching me from my thoughts.

I hold the plastic cup to her, and she dips her corn dog into the mustard as we walk. When she takes a big bite, I grin. It only took two weeks to put weight on Twiggy, but slowly, she began to fill out her clothes. Her slight frame became sexy and slightly curvaceous.

"Mustard," she says again, never losing her stride.

We've become accustomed to our walking dinners, and I think she secretly looks forward to them. You wouldn't think so with the annoyed sound that rushes from her as she hands me her now empty stick. But I know the truth and bite back my smile as I take it from her to drop it into the cup.

"Any big clients on the schedule for tonight?" I ask as we near the bar.

She shrugs her shoulders. "Gus didn't have anything written down, which is really weird. I always work Sundays."

I sense that something is off, so I escort her up the stairs and into the tattoo shop.

"Lark? I didn't expect you in tonight," Gus says in surprise upon seeing us.

She flicks her gaze to me in confusion. Fuck if I know what's going on. I just shrug my shoulders.

"Gus, why wouldn't I be in? I always work on Sundays," she snaps.

"But it's the eighteenth and you never show up," he gulps as if his words will damage her.

Fuck.

The eighteenth.

His words do damage her and the gasp that escapes her is the indication that they do.

Her purse falls from her shoulder and hits the tile floor with a clatter. Shit—she's going down. I drop the cup and slip my arms around her before she meets the same demise as her purse.

"How could I?" she murmurs with so much self-hate that I cringe.

"Lark," I whisper into her hair.

"Get me out of here," she hisses.

Gus shakes his head and sends me a sympathetic look. He's used to her unstable behavior.

"Can you walk?" I question before I release her from my grasp.

She nods, so I reluctantly let her go and pick her purse up off the floor. I expect her to go sit down, but instead, she turns on her heel and bolts out the door. With a groan, I trot after her. When I reach the landing at the bottom, I get a glimpse of her brown hair flowing wildly behind her as she slides through the door of the bar.

I push the door open and stalk after her, carrying her purse as if it holds a bomb. Several patrons toss amused looks my way, but I ignore them. She's hopped up onto a barstool and already ordered a drink by the time I take the seat beside her.

"Care to explain the eighteenth?" I question.

The bartender lines up three shots of vodka in front of her. I steal one and toss it back before she can argue. She doesn't need to get shit-faced. She needs to talk to me.

When she ignores my question, I think about what Pallas said when I went to see him on Wednesday.

"She's unstable." His cigar wiggles in his mouth as he says the words.

"Unstable doesn't mean evil, Pallas."

His eyes narrow, and for the first time ever, he removes the cigar. "Listen, son. She is a job. Her file dates back to when she was twelve years old and began visiting cemeteries for fun. She has a dark side—a side you haven't clearly witnessed yet. Lark Miller is not your friend. Lark Miller cannot be saved. There is a destiny to be fulfilled. There is a pair of wings waiting with your name on them."

I think about the permanent ones on my skin. The ones she gave me. The ones they'll never be able to take away even when I retire years from now.

"I've been careful. I became her friend so that I could keep an eye on her at all times," I assure him.

He grins and puts his beloved cigar back between his teeth. "You'll make it to the end of your assignment and you'll join the Seraph Guardians. I know you can do this, Alpha."

The pride on his face is evident, and I realize that, besides Omega, Pallas is the closest thing to family I can remember. He's like a father to me. I won't let him down.

The problem is that I don't want to let Lark down either. Something niggles in my brain and whispers, "Something isn't right." I can't put a finger on it, but I'll find out.

By the time I shake the memory away, she's already ordered three more shots. I manage to steal one more before she finishes the other two.

"Asshole," she groans but doesn't do much else in lieu of arguing.

"Time to go, Twiggy," I grumble.

Her face turns to regard me, and I see heartache. I also see that her bitchy walls are down and nothing but utter despair remains.

"I miss them. Both of them."

Big, fat tears roll down her cheeks and she sniffles loudly. I haven't slept in her bed again since that night she broke down, but tonight, I'm not leaving her side. I may not know what's going on in that head of hers, but I can't have her being reckless and hurting herself.

"Come on. I'm taking you home," I tell her as I slide off the stool. "Climb on." I turn my back to her and point at my shoulders.

I expect her to laugh at me.

I expect to be told to fuck off.

I don't expect slender fingers to skim up my shoulders without hesitation.

"Don't forget your purse," I instruct.

She slips it on her arm while I bend over. Her arms wrap around my neck, and her legs hook my waist as I return to an upright position. When I turn toward the bartender to pay her tab, he just shakes his head. I nod my thanks and bounce out of the bar with the skinniest, most unusual woman I've ever met latched on my back.

As soon as we hit the warm Los Angeles night air, I adjust my grip on her legs so she doesn't fall off. I'd be a fucking liar if I said I didn't enjoy the way her lips and nose are pressed into the hair on the back of my head. Awareness skitters through every nerve ending as I realize her legs are spread deliciously around me. I don't press her to talk but instead remain as her quiet companion the entire fifteen-minute walk back to our apartment building.

She attempts to ease herself off me when the apartment building comes into view, but I grip her tight. I'm not letting go of her until I have her naked in bed.

My dick hardens at the thought of touching her naked, and I force the thoughts from my head. Every now and again, images of her body creep into my head. Those luscious tits. Her cute, round ass. She'll always be a temptation, but I won't ever give in. A little over two months from now and I won't be burdened with worrying about her.

You'll miss her.

I push the door open and leave that thought outside. As I reach the stairs, I give her thighs a squeeze.

"Hold on, Twiggy, I'm taking you for a ride."

She lets out a squeal of delight when I bounce her hard as I practically fly upstairs. Loud music is once again pounding behind Pedro's door. Omega and Lovenia spend a good portion of their time over there when they aren't fucking like animals in my apartment. He seems like he has it all under control, but I have a feeling Lovenia has something up her sleeve. Just yesterday, I warned him that she was there to rattle us and she was getting to him hardcore. He flipped me off and reminded me that Pedro was still alive. I told him that maybe they shouldn't sleep together, and he said that he'll fuck her until the day he earns his SG wings. I'm not sure what'll happen after that.

When I finally set her down in front of her door, she fishes the keys out of her bag. Then she hands them to me and I unlock the door for her. The alcohol has taken a slight effect because she wobbles as she walks in. For Christmas, I'll buy her a fucking helmet.

She makes a crooked beeline toward her bedroom and once inside, heads toward the closet. The box.

"Want me to get it down for you?" I question as I point to it.

Her head snaps to mine. "No. You can leave now, Al."

And I slip. *On purpose.* "Alpha."

Her eyes narrow at me. "What?"

"My name is Alpha."

Plump lips pop open in surprise. Her lips are perfect.

"Alpha. What exactly does that mean? What kind of mother names her kid Alpha?" Her sadness is momentarily gone as she studies me.

"I don't know my mother."

More confusion. "Who are you, Al?"

"I could ask you the same thing, Lark."

Her teeth bite her bottom lip—the bottom lip I'd love to be right about now. "Alpha? Seriously, that has to be the most god-awful name I've ever heard."

I chuckle, but my eyes never leave her mouth. Stepping toward her, I say, "And Lark? That name's pretty terrible as well, babe."

Her green eyes flicker with amusement, and a small smile tugs at her lips. I'll take it.

"My mom wanted Clark. I was supposed to be a boy. They dropped the 'c' and voila. Lark was born."

I take another step and brush a long, brown strand out of her eyes. Those eyes should always be visible for my viewing.

"I'm glad you were born," I tell her honestly.

Jade eyes sparkle at my words. "I'm glad this world has an Alpha. It would be a much hungrier world with him." Another small smile.

Her smiles do something to me. When she smiles, joy fills every ounce of my being. This is exactly why I don't want to ask her my next question. I hate the idea of breaking this moment, but I need to know.

"What's up with the eighteenth, Twiggy?"

Her eyes dull before she looks down at her feet. Sliding a hand under her chin, I tilt her head up so I can see her.

"Tell me, woman."

With a quiver of her lips, she shakes her head. She won't tell me, but I can see the hurt written all over her face. Dipping my mouth to hers, I graze my lips across her perfect ones. A hint of mustard invades my senses. Such a temptation.

I will kiss her. Kissing isn't against the rules. I can still do my job after one kiss. She needs something to take the tears away. A small kiss will help that ache in her heart. This has nothing to do with me. I will keep her whole and alive for a little over two more months. Kissing her is a strategy.

I've convinced myself now.

Leaning in ever so slightly, I press my lips to hers. My tongue doesn't enter her mouth and hers doesn't breach mine. We simply connect with our lips. Her softness of her kiss is such a contrast of the jagged edges that are her. Flashes of her soul flood my mind. Dark. Then light. Dark again. And, finally, a ray of light. I see pain. Love. Hate. Hope. Fear. I see blue eyes and coffins. I see headstones and roses. I see positive pregnancy tests. I see blood. Dog tags. Tears. Oreos. Darkness. Light.

Once I wrench my lips away from hers, my eyes dart around as I realize the intensity of our kiss. She's still every bit a mystery, but my soul has locked with hers in some way I don't understand. I feel a fierce protectiveness over her that goes beyond a job.

She's mine.

Chapter Ten

Lark

WHO IS THIS man? He breaks our kiss and regards me angrily. Like I bewitched him into kissing me. I didn't ask for his delicious lips on mine. I didn't ask for him to follow me around like a bad habit.

"Who are you, Lark Miller?" he questions again.

It would seem he wants to know about me as much as I'd like to know about him. The man who works for the "government" yet never works. The man who doesn't have one imperfection on his body. The man who just showed up out of nowhere to suddenly look after me for no reason.

So show him.

I meet his stare, but I don't answer him. After grabbing the hem of my T-shirt, I peel it from my body and reveal my bare tits. His eyes darken when they drop to my chest, but then he drags them back to mine.

"What are you doing?"

"I'm showing you my story."

He nods and swallows a lump in his throat as I unbutton my jeans and push them down my thighs before standing in nothing but a red pair of panties. His gaze drink up every bit of me.

"Food looks good on you, Twiggy." He winks.

My body responds to his words, but I attempt to ignore his compliment. I've made the decision to in some way explain myself to him, so he won't distract me now that I've begun.

"This was my first one. I was eighteen. How fucking appropriate." I laugh, but it's hollow.

He drops to his knees in front of me and strokes the words on my hip bone.

Death is only the beginning.

Black eyes fly to mine in question.

I shrug. "So I thought."

That night, when the needle pierced my ivory flesh, I knew. I simply knew that every part of my life would be documented in some way on my skin. I knew that, no matter what I couldn't say, my skin would tell the story.

And oh what a beautiful story it was.

Was.

"What's this one?" he questions, pointing to a pink bow near my belly button.

Tears fill my eyes as I push his finger away. "Not yet." I turn away from him and crawl onto the bed.

The eighteenth is so incredibly exhausting for me. As I lie down on my back on top of the covers, I watch the beautiful man in my room. When he rips his shirt off, I get a glimpse of the angel wings on his back. He truly does look like some badass angel. I swallow as he unbuckles his belt and sheds his body of his jeans. This would be the second time I've seen him in only his boxers.

And oh what a glorious sight it is.

The bed sinks down as he crawls in next to me. His heavy hand finds the words of my first tattoo, and he traces them with his strong finger.

"I'm ready for more," he urges me. He props up on his elbow so he can see my face, his dark eyes hiding the mysteries that are him. Will I ever find them out?

I trace my finger along the knuckle he's using to skim over my tattoo. Then he slides it down to the inside of my thigh. More words.

Smiles are evil.

He scoots down along the bed so he can look at it. His hot breath tickles the small patch of hair just under the lace of my panties.

"Smiles are evil." He looks over at me and gives me the goofiest lopsided grin he can muster. And holy shit—it is the very reason I got this tattoo. "You're a weird one, Lark."

I swat at him and he chuckles. Smiles are evil, but that laugh is the devil.

"You're weirder, Alpha."

Alpha.

"What does it mean?" he questions. This time when his finger traces the flesh near the most sensitive part of my entire body, I nearly buck right off the bed.

"Stop," I murmur even though my body begs him not to.

His tracing stops, but he doesn't move his finger.

"I met a boy," I admit. "And when he smiled, my life began."

He turns his head to me and grins again. "I like this story."

A tear rolls out, and I look toward the top shelf of my closet. "I don't." My silence stretches between us, but he doesn't push. Finally, I sigh and swallow my tears. "He made me forget. With one smile, he became my whole world. Always by my side. He was my best friend. My only friend. My reason for living."

A bitter thought creeps deep into my soul. *Just like Alpha.*

"I'm glad you had him," he says.

I'm glad I had him too.

Too bad it didn't last.

"What happened?"

A sob escapes me. "One day, it happened. We fell madly in love, and it was terrible."

Would I do it all over again? Of course I would.

"Terrible? How? Was he mean to you? Did he hurt you?" he growls menacingly as his black eyes meet mine.

In this moment, I know deep down in my soul that Alpha would protect me with his life. He came out of nowhere, but he somehow claimed me as his own.

For three months. Less now, actually.

Time is ticking.

"He hurt me. He left me. And he never came back."

Alpha's fingers trail up my body, circle my belly button, and skim over my ribs just under my breasts. My breath hitches.

"If you were mine, I'd never leave you," he murmurs as he traces the curve.

I slide my hand down to cover his. "I'll never be yours. Or anyone's for that matter. Besides, it wasn't his fault."

His large hand splays across my ribs, and he kisses one of the stars between my breasts. Star number one to be exact. A never-ending ache that only hides from time to time slices through my heart.

"What's this one?" His question is mostly breath against flesh. Against the star that protects my heart.

"One year after. I got this star one year after my world turned upside down. I was his star, he said. I fell right from the sky and into his life."

You're a star, Lar.

"Then why'd he leave you?" he asks, this time pressing his lips against my skin.

My body shivers at his touch. It feels wrong—being here with this man, talking about another.

"He was stolen from me. But before he left, he gave me a gift. And, Alpha, it was perfect," I whimper. The tears silently slide down my cheeks while the hysterics stay lodged in my throat.

Awareness hits him as he trails his finger to the pink bow on my belly. "This was your gift." He doesn't ask. He figured it out on his own.

"Yep. So beautiful. My favorite gift," I tell him sadly.

"What happened, Lark?"

Dog tags. Folded flag. Oorah. Shower. Blood. Gone.

"They took my heart, Al. My little black rock inside my body had become something because of him. And when he left me, I had her. Then she left me too. Together, they left this fucking life that I only lived for them. Together, they went to some happy place. Without me," I sob. "Goddammit, Alpha, I want to see them again."

My tears become a snotty mess as I cry for my sweet husband. As I cry for our daughter who came too early and was gone just as quickly. I cry for the woman I never got to be, for the woman I have become.

His warmth covers me as he places kisses all over me as if to kiss the holes in my soul. "I'm so sorry, Lark. You're just a sad girl. Broken. You don't deserve this."

I whimper when his lips find my neck, and my legs wrap around his waist. This man on top of me has found a way into my heart. There might only be a tiny sliver left, but with each corn dog and smile, he found a way in.

He'll leave too. Time's ticking, Lark.

My thoughts dissipate when I feel his erection pressing against the part of me that throbs to be touched. A part of me that hasn't been touched since *him.*

"You're the biggest fucking temptation I've ever encountered, sweet Lark," he whispers against my neck.

His hands are tangled in my hair, but he doesn't slow the thrusting of his body against mine. Only the small scrap of my panties and the cotton of his boxers separate the heat of each of our bodies.

"Alpha, you distract me too," I admit.

I'd nearly forgotten the eighteenth—the day my husband was blown to smithereens by a roadside bomb in Afghanistan. Two months later, to the exact date, I began hemorrhaging in the shower—the day I lost my baby and nearly my uterus in the process.

The eighteenth is significant. The eighteenth is gutting. The eighteenth is unforgettable.

"You need to live, honey," Mom says as she sips her coffee.

The noises in the coffee shop grate on my nerves. Her words *grate on my nerves.*

"I think that ship has sailed," I snarl as I push my cooling coffee away from me. The smell suddenly disgusts me.

"Lark, I think you need to go back and see Dr. Walsh. You're not well. Your father and I are worried about you. It's almost been a year," she whispers as if she's afraid to remind me.

Too late.

"Mom, this isn't something I can just forget. I lost my husband. My baby!" I shriek.

She holds her hands up in a comforting move, but I am not fucking comforted. I'm furious.

"What's the big deal? Why are you so hell-bent on making me forget? They were my life! I am dead now! Dead," I hiss. My chest heaves

wildly.

"Honey—"

"Don't. Just leave me the fuck alone, Mom."

"Lark?" Alpha questions, tearing me from my thoughts.

My eyes find his dark ones, which are now staring at me as he attempts to climb right into my head and figure me out.

"What?"

"I want you," he grumbles as if the very thought annoys him.

He pushes hard against my pussy, and I cry out against his lips, which are hovering over mine. My body wants him too. Whimpers spill out of my trembling lips as he presses his dick against me in just the right way that makes my head dizzy.

"I haven't been touched in so long," I admit. "Since him."

His lips press against mine for the second time tonight. This kiss has the same effect, and I lose my mind. My fingers find his unruly hair and grab two handfuls. With a sudden need, I pull him deeper into my kiss.

And then it happens.

His tongue enters my mouth and I lose all sense of reality.

Alpha.

Chapter Eleven

Alpha

ALPHA. LARK. ALPHA. Lark. Alpha. Lark.

This is bad.

But oh so good.

The first kiss we shared was a glimpse into her soul. Her past. Her pain.

This kiss is yet another glimpse into her soul. This time, fire and heat. And me.

"Make love to me," she begs between kisses.

One of the biggest rules flashes like crazy in my head.

Thou shalt not fornicate with final assignment. If Minder fornicates with final assignment, they will be terminated from the program and banished from HEA Corp property. HEL will become administrator over failed Minder, whom shalt now be called Reaper.

Fuck!

"Make love to me." This time more of a command.

My dick begs, too. I'm only holding on to one tiny shred of sanity. What we're doing is so wrong. She's my job, not my girlfriend. In just over two months, she'll be gone. They'll take her—to Hell.

The thought of her in eternal, torturous agony sends rage swirling in my veins. She can't die. She can't go to fucking Hell. It doesn't make sense. Then a dark thought enters my mind.

I'll protect her.

Forever.

"Alpha, please," she whimpers.

Shit, I'll never be able to tell her no.

I untangle one of my hands from her hair and dive in for more of her mouth. My hand finds her panties, and we have to break momentarily for me to rip them from her body. They're made of lace and nothing, so they disappear in an instant.

"Lark," I groan against her mouth as I reach into my boxers and pull my dick out. "This changes everything."

"I'm sorry," she says. I'm not sure if she's telling me or her dead husband.

"I'm not." I make that final decision. The decision that burns a mark so black on my soul that I almost cry out from the pain of it.

With one hard thrust, I plunge deep inside my sweet Lark.

Everything else around me disappears. The only thing that exists is her. This perfect, beautiful, dark angel belongs to me. I know I've just broken a serious law. And I'm unsure what the repercussions will be.

Right now, though, I don't care. Right now, all that matters is her. Her tight, hot body hugs my cock with each thrust into her. Fingernails claw at the wings they can't take away from me. As I push myself as deep as I can into her, our souls bind together.

Connor.

The thought unlocks some tiny mystery in my head. A single memory. My name.

"Alpha!" she shrieks as her body shudders beneath me. Her pussy clenches around my dick so fiercely that it pulls the orgasm right out of me. I come deep inside her, and it's perfect.

We're perfect together.

This is my destiny.

Lark Miller.

Not a job. *Mine.*

I collapse onto her tiny frame and lose myself in her neck. She now smells sweeter. Her skin feels softer. I'll never let her go.

As her delicate fingers stroke my wings, my heart soars. My job doesn't matter. My destiny doesn't matter. Only Lark matters.

"Let's run away," I murmur against the shell of her ear.

Her pussy clenches around my soft cock, and it twitches back to life.

"And leave this grand life behind, Al?" she giggles.

Smiles are evil. Her laugh is heavenly.

I begin pumping into her again. Her body is so perfect that I want to live here forever. Surely we can exist like this, neither of us needing anything but the taste of the other.

"What are you doing to me?" she pants out as I plunge into her.

"I'm making you mine forever," I answer and devour her lips.

Her moans and whimpers are fuel, and I don't stop. I can't stop.

"Oh, God!" she screams with another orgasm.

I growl and suck her lip into my mouth as I release inside her once again. My heart and soul pour into her until I've given it all to her.

"I think my real name is Connor," I confess against her mouth. The name feels foreign on my tongue, but I feel connected to it nonetheless.

Suddenly, the warm, squirming body beneath me goes cold. Her finally relaxed body becomes rigid.

Time freezes for one long moment before she explodes.

"Get off me!" she seethes, her tone so filled with hate.

I scramble off her like a fucking pussy. What did I do wrong?

Naked and her arms flailing, she rolls out of the bed and turns to face me. "I should kill you. Get out of my house and don't ever come back!"

I stare at her in confusion. Thoughts of the file hit me.

Unstable.

Drug addict.

Evil.

"Lark," I say in an attempt to calm her.

Her full tits bounce as she storms over to my clothes on the floor. Then she bends over and starts heaving them at me. When she throws my shoes, I pounce out of the bed toward her.

"Don't you fucking touch me, asshole. Get out!" Her eyes are wild and lost.

The woman I just gave my soul to is insane.

"I'm sorry. I don't know what I did, Lark. Don't push me away. You don't understand what I've given up for you."

When crazed eyes meet mine, I know there's no negotiation. So I dress quickly and storm out of her apartment without a glance in her direction. Then I sleep propped up against the door of her apartment in the scummy hallway.

"Wake up, Al."

My stiff neck aches when I blink open my eyes and attempt to follow the source of the kicking against my thigh. Steel-toed boots. Omega.

"I fucked up, man," I confess with a dry, raspy voice.

His brown eyes peer down at me under his girly-looking lashes. "Is she dead?"

Anger blasts through my body. "What? Fuck that! No, she isn't dead, and she won't die on my watch," I snarl. My body has come back to life, so I climb to my feet and glare at him.

He folds his muscular arms across his chest and watches me. "Then how did you fuck up, Al?"

I run a hand through my inky hair and push thoughts of my soul mate from my head. Leaning forward, I whisper, "I slept with her. Twice."

Now it's Omega's turn to get angry. And he fucking detonates. "What the fuck, man? Are you kidding me right now? Do you even understand what will happen to you if they find out? They will know. They always know, Alpha."

I groan because I know. Their sources are everywhere.

"What do I do?" I question as pussy tears sting my eyes. I don't want to be away from her for one second. I can't.

"We have to tell Pallas."

Pallas.

Fuck.

"No, Omega. Please. Maybe I can figure this out. Besides, she hates me now anyway. Maybe they won't find out."

"Don't be stupid, man. They will find out. Maybe they'll just put you back into training. They would be lucky to have you as an SG, but maybe you need a little more time. It will be better to come clean and take a lesser punishment. I need you, brother."

And I need him too.

But Lark?

I can't fucking breathe without her. She infected my very being, and I'll waste away into the Earth without her. I would be nothing.

"What's going on, boys?" a sultry voice asks. Lovenia.

Omega spins on his foot and faces the dark-haired demon who's sauntering toward us. Her lips are painted bright red, an amused, brunette brow is raised, and a smirk plays on her lips as she approaches.

"Nothing," I spit out quickly.

Her laughter is like jingling bells. So sweet. Too bad I know her kind. They are not sweet.

"Alpha, don't lie. It's not becoming of your kind." She smiles as she steps around Omega.

His hand slides around her middle and he possessively pulls her back to his chest. When neither of us responds, she grins at me.

"I can keep a secret. In fact, I could probably help you. As long as the girl in there didn't die, your secret stays here. I'm their link, you know. I've been assigned to you both."

I sense deception, but I feel lulled into her charms. Just like Omega has been.

"I'll bite. What do I need to do?"

Her smile spreads beautifully across her face. "Meet my boss."

Omega and I exchange glances.

"Love?" he questions her.

She raises a slender arm and threads her fingers into his hair. "Yes, baby?"

"Don't betray me or my brother. If you do, that will end us," he warns.

When her eyes flash to mine, I see the briefest flash of something. But she quickly schools it away before I can figure out her intentions.

"Just meet your boss? That's all you want? You'll keep this little tidbit of information from our superiors?" I'm mystified. Lovenia has always been a friend, even though we're destined to be enemies, but this seems huge.

"Of course, darling. Just a meeting, Alpha. But both of you. He wants to meet the famous Alpha and Omega." She bats her lashes at me.

I raise a brow in question to Omega, and he nods. He would do anything for me.

"Set it up, Love. Thank you so much," I rush out in relief.

She breaks free from Omega and hugs me tight.

Why do I feel like I just made a deal with the devil?

Chapter Twelve

Lark

ONE WEEK.

A whole week of avoiding him.

Fucking Alpha with the tongue of the devil.

He still followed me around like a lost puppy and gave me food, but I refused to look at him or even speak to him. I bared my soul to him and he said things to me that broke me again. Everything that was a part of my old life sat up in that box in my closet. There must have been some piece of information that showed him a glimpse into my past. Whatever joke he was playing at was fucked up.

After I dress in a pair of jean shorts, my combat boots, and a black tank that says, *I hate people,* I climb up in my closet and retrieve my box. I still have some time before I have to go to see the kids for Poem Day. The box is heavy—just like my heart—but I clutch it fiercely and hop back down with it. Once I've set it on the bed, I flip the flaps open and peer inside.

Folded Marine Corps T-shirt. *No name.*

Framed sonogram. *No name.*

Photo album. *Fuck. I'm not sure I can even look through it to check.*

Jewelry box. *Contents: two wedding bands, gold cross. No name.*

Folded American flag. *No name.*

Of the things I kept, the only things that fit inside this box, nothing has my husband's name on it.

With a gulp and tears threatening to spill, I pull the photo album out. The first page guts me.

Me and him. I'm dressed like a fucking goth queen and he looks like the boy next door in his white T-shirt and winning smile. I may be glaring at the camera, but my eyes are smiling. One corner of my lips is turned up, too. His muscled arm is slung casually over my shoulder. I remember that day clearly.

"Sir, can you take our picture please?" he asks a man jogging by.

The man grins, not at all bothered by us, and snaps our photo. Then he jogs away.

"You're my girlfriend now, Lar," he tells me as he admires the picture on his phone.

I raise my eyebrow at him, but my heart is pounding happily at his words.

"Is that so, Army boy?" I tease.

"Marines," he growls. "Oorah."

I playfully roll my eyes at him.

"You're so fucking sassy, woman," he mutters in a tone that makes me think he enjoys my sassiness a little too much. My suspicions are confirmed when he leans in and presses a hungry kiss to my lips. A needy mewl escapes me as I run my fingers through his blond hair and tug him to me, kissing him deeper. Needing to be closer to him, I straddle his hips on the bench in the park and grind into him.

"And"—he momentarily breaks away from my lips—"that means we have to do something to celebrate."

When blue eyes twinkle mischievously, I know. As I slowly push my pussy against him in the park, I know. Tonight, in his apartment, we'll make love. I'll lose my virginity at the Granny old age of eighteen to my sweet boyfriend.

"I love you," I tell him suddenly.

He grins. "I know you do."

I lightheartedly swat at him. He's been telling me for two months that he loves me, and I've been telling him that he's insane. But he's right. I've loved him since the moment he smiled at me while jogging past my front porch one day. That smile. This boy. They've owned my heart since then, and I hope they never give it back.

As the memories fade, I realize I'm sobbing. One picture. I can't look at two hundred more. I just can't. I attempt to recall if any picture has his name on it, but I don't remember there being one.

Needing to feel close to him, I pull my necklace out the jewelry box with shaking fingers and manage to slide the long chain over my head. Once I tuck it inside my tank top and between my breasts, I pat it lovingly. With a sigh, I close the lid to the box of memories and scoop my purse up off the dresser. Then I haul ass out of my apartment, having made the split decision to talk to Alpha. I need fucking answers.

When I fling my door open, I expect to see him there. Waiting. Like always. But he's not there.

A sudden, painful pang rips through me, and I kick the wall. The drywall in the hallway buckles against the toe of my boot.

"Pretty girls shouldn't kick ugly walls," a feminine voice chirps.

My eyes skim down the hallway to see stupid Lovenia once again sneaking out of Pedro's apartment and heading toward Omar and Alpha's.

Skank-ass ho.

"Should pretty girls kick ugly sluts instead?" I snap. I am not in the mood for her sugary bullshit today.

Her eyes widen in surprise, but a naughty grin curls her lips up. "Aren't you a little feisty this morning? Where's your boyfriend?"

Boyfriend.

"He. Is. Not. My. Boyfriend."

"Yet." She smiles knowingly as she raps on their door.

Before I can argue, the door swings open and Omar barrels out, gathering her in his arms along the way. He hugs her so tight that I think he'll break her. When she makes eye contact with me over his shoulder, I glower back at her. Ignoring me, she flicks her eyes over to Pedro's door and then raises her finger to her pursed lips as she tells me to be quiet about what I saw.

I give her a finger back—the middle one.

Finally, Omar releases her and sends a look my way. There's sadness in his eyes, and I feel guilty.

"Where's Al?" I demand as I walk toward them.

His brows furrow angrily at me. "Don't you think you've done enough damage, Lark?"

Whoa. Wasn't expecting him to lash out on me.

My hands find my hips and I glare at him. "Where?"

He rolls his eyes at my blatant ignoring of his rude question. "He's sick."

Sick?

My heart clenches painfully in my chest. "What's wrong?"

I attempt to sidestep him and go into his apartment, but his massive frame fills the doorway, stopping me.

"I don't know. Maybe he's suffering from a broken heart. Look, things would go a lot smoother if you would just continue to leave him the fuck alone. You treated him like trash and ignored him for an entire fucking week. The point was made. You're not interested. So please stop dragging him along. I won't watch my best friend be toyed with by a simple girl."

Simple girl compared to sophisticated woman like Lovenia? *Fuck you, Omar.*

"Out of my way, asshole," I threaten. I don't care what the hell he thinks about me. I have questions for Alpha, and Omar's burly ass won't stop me.

When Lovenia giggles from behind me, I have to physically hold back from punching her in her goddamned nose. With a grunt, Omar steps out of my way and pulls her back into his arms. I ignore the smacking of their lips as they kiss and stride through the apartment until I find his room. The bed is empty, so I walk toward the bathroom.

The sight there scares me.

Alpha stands in front of the mirror in just a pair of jeans, his shoulders hunched. His tattooed angel wings even appear to be sagging. Black hair is a big fucking mess all over his head as if he didn't even bother to shower today. As I approach, I can see his reflection in the mirror—the scruff on his face is darker and thicker. His black eyes almost seem grey. The normally olive tone to his skin seems ashen.

"What's wrong with you?" I whisper. I came in here angry and upset, but now, I'm just worried.

The man who always looks after me needs looking after.

He doesn't answer me as he continues to stare at his reflection.

When he doesn't respond again, I slide my arms around his middle. His skin is ice cold, so I squeeze tight and attempt to warm him, pressing my lips right between his wings.

"Alpha, come lie down. Let me take care of you," I whisper against his back.

No response. He's borderline catatonic. Why in the fuck has Omar not taken him to the emergency room?

I peek around his shoulder and see his reflection again. Self-loathing. Defeat.

I don't fucking think so.

Even in his statuesque state, he's still built like a brick wall. It takes some yanking on my part, but I finally get him to break his hold and he stumbles back. Once I have momentum working with me, I pull him out of the bathroom and toward the bed. When the back of my knees hit the bed, I fall and bring him with me.

"Holy shit, you're heavy," I groan as I attempt to push him off. It takes some maneuvering, but eventually, I manage to topple him over.

"As fucking hilarious as this is, I don't want you to hurt my friend. Move, Twiggy," Omar chuckles from behind me.

I roll my eyes at him but move out of the way and watch in awe as he lifts Alpha as if he weighs nothing and lays him down on the pillow with his legs stretched out along the bed. What took him three seconds and zero energy would have taken me at least thirty minutes and I would have passed out after.

"Thanks," I mutter as he leaves me to his friend. Then I kick off my boots, clamber onto the bed, and straddle his waist. "Al, what's wrong? You're scaring the shit out of me."

As I lean forward and bring my face close to his so I can get his attention, the cross slides out of my shirt and down around his neck. He flinches. When he begins blinking in confusion, I freeze and study is eyes. Slowly, they begin to darken as color returns to his face.

Thank fuck.

"Lark," he murmurs, running his palms up my bare thighs.

A small whimper escapes me at his touch, but I quickly push it away, remembering why I am here.

"I'm here. What happened?" I demand as I finally lift away from him.

Our eyes never leave one another's as his thumbs circle the insides of my thighs, dangerously high up my legs, and I ignore the wash of dizziness.

"I'm allergic to mirrors."

Some truth, some lie. This man is so damn weird.

One of his hands leaves my thigh to reach for my breasts. My body snubs the screams from the sane part of my mind and shudders at the thought of him touching me intimately again. I actually sigh in frustration when his fingers probe the cross hanging in front of them instead.

"This is beautiful, Lark." He continues to finger it but doesn't let go. The circling of his thumb on my leg creeps higher and higher until I can feel it graze my panty line just under my shorts.

Holy shit. Get your shit together, Lark.

I came here to talk to him. To question him. So why has my mind suddenly gone blank? Why is the only thing my mind can focus on the way his thumb has now connected with my clit?

Gasps come from me as he innocently massages my throbbing pleasure spot over my panties. I feel myself growing wetter for him with each lazy circle. Both of us are frozen—the only things moving are his thumb and my chest as I struggle to breathe.

"Come for me, sweet Lark," he rumbles—so low that I can barely hear him.

My eyes slam shut as my body seizes in ecstasy. I cry out his name and let him touch my sensitive pussy until I collapse onto his chest, completely spent from my orgasm. His thumb leaves my skin and he holds me in a tight hug.

Together, we lie in each other's arms for some time, neither of us speaking. In a perfect world, I would live here. I would never need words or nourishment or sleep. Just his scent and safe arms.

"Al, we need to talk," I tell him reluctantly.

Lifting up slightly, I look into his coal-black eyes. His skin has returned to its olive glow.

"Are you still wet?" he questions with a raised brow and a half-cocked grin that makes me crazy for him.

"You're so distracting," I pout but find myself slowly rubbing my spread legs against his erect cock.

"Baby, you are the biggest distraction I've ever met and I can't be happier about it," he chuckles.

My body aches to have him one more time. What if, after we talk, it is the end for us? What if I don't like his explanation? Will I ever have a chance to be with him again?

Probably not.

Just one more time, and then we can discuss why he said the name Connor.

One.

More.

Time.

My eyes must beg him to ask the question again, because he does and I'm too fucking happy to answer him.

"Are you still wet?"

"Why don't you find out, big boy?"

Just one more time won't hurt.

Chapter Thirteen

Alpha

THIS WOMAN IS killing me.

Literally.

I will be dead—and soon—because of her.

Because of this tattooed, dark-haired vixen, my life is over.

Done.

Finito.

Over.

Do I care?

Not one fucking bit. She's worth it, and I'd do it over and over again. I'd forsake my career, my destiny, *my life* just to spend one second more with her. Of course, I say this now, having not yet been caught, but I know this to be true.

I will find a way to be with her for as long as I can.

Her green eyes are liquid lust as she grabs the hem of her wicked tank top and yanks it away from her body. Today, she's wearing a black bra, and even though I want to see those pink, suckable nipples, I'm very much enjoying the view of her full tits spilling out of the top of her bra.

This woman is gorgeous. So fucking beautiful. Mine.

But for how long?

As long as *she'll* have me. And as long as *they'll* let me have her.

My hands find her hips and I urge her to push harder against my dick. The clothes between us seem like brick fucking walls. I need her skin on mine. Now.

As she reaches behind her back to unclasp her bra, I set to unbuttoning her jean shorts. Once she frees her breasts and tosses her bra away, she eyes me with one brow raised.

"This is going to be pretty difficult with clothes on," she smiles.

I growl and roll her underneath me in the middle of the bed. "We better fix that, then."

She giggles when I unzip her shorts and pull them down with her panties. I climb off the bed away from her and shed myself of my jeans. The boxers fall shortly thereafter, and then I'm back in bed between her legs—this time, with my mouth.

"I need to taste you, sweet Lark," I murmur as my warning right before I dive in.

The moment my tongue slides between the lips of her pussy, she arches her back off of the bed. "Holy shit!" she cries out.

My hair gets tangled in her grasp, but it doesn't slow my roll. I taste her like there's no tomorrow—because there might not be. I pleasure her as if she's my first and last—because she will be. I nibble her as if she's my last meal—I can certainly hope.

With one hand holding her hip in place while I give her the best pleasure of her life, I slip a finger inside her wet opening. She's so hot, tight, and perfect.

I curve my finger up and search for a place sure to make her crazy. The moment I find that elusive spot, she screams so loudly that I'm sure the neighbors will complain. Oh wait—she *is* the neighbor and I don't hear her complaining.

I don't have to circle her sensitive skin with my tongue for very long before she completely and utterly unravels. Her body quivers and violently shakes as she gives in to the sheer pleasure of another orgasm. The first one I gave her moments ago was sweet. This one was decadent and sinful.

"You're so wet and ready for me," I growl as I remove my finger from her body.

Her response is a ragged sigh. Green eyes are hidden behind her eyelids, and suddenly, I need to see her.

"Lark, look at me please." I'm not sure where my abrupt insecurity comes from, but I have an overwhelming desire for her to want me just as badly as I want her. To make this all make sense. This can't be one-sided. That would be the ultimate death for me.

She lazily blinks her eyes open and finds mine. So perfect.

"Do you want this? Me?" I question as I cover her body with mine. My dick, hard as stone, rests between us.

She raises her head in search for my lips, which will taste like her. I can't kiss her until I know though.

"Lar, please," I whisper against her eager lips.

"Yes, okay? I want this. You. Us. Now fuck me."

This time, my eyes close. She's Heaven and Hell in one delicious package.

When my eyes finally fly back open, I meet her pleading, green ones. Then I grab my aching cock and tease the part of her that drips for me.

"You're mine, baby. Forever," I tell her.

She bites her lip, seemingly uncertain, but nods.

I'll take that as a deal.

I slam into her tight heat so hard that she screams even louder than before. Last week, we made love, but this morning, we're fucking. And holy shit it's amazing. It seems like it's been an eternity since the last time I was inside her.

When our lips find one another again, I kiss her hard as I'm taking her. My tongue punishes her in a way that seems more like a painful reward. We bite. We suck. We take. We own.

"Oh, God!" she moans into my mouth. Her body is doing its telltale quivering, so I know she's coming. When her pussy clamps down on my dick, I lose it. All of it. My release pours into her long and strong. I don't stop my thrusting until I'm sure she's completely filled with me. Only me.

"I love you," I murmur and suck on her bottom lip.

Her tiny palms find my chest, and she slightly pushes me up away from her. "You're insane," she breathes out against my mouth.

I expect her to be angry, but her eyes tear up again.

"How can you love me, Al? You barely know me."

But I do know her. I feel like I've always known her. Like I always will.

"I just do. I knew the moment I laid eyes on you."

I rest my cheek against her neck and physically stay connected with her. Her fingertips stroke my wings, and it feels amazing. Who needs Heaven when she's already in your arms? Who needs wings when you have an angel in your grasp? Who needs a career when your purpose is right in front of you?

"Al?" she finally murmurs, her fingers never stopping their movements.

"Yes, sweet Lark?"

"We need to talk."

I sigh. "I know." Lifting up on my elbows, I look down at her.

"How do you know that name? It's nowhere in my apartment, yet you know the name of my dead husband."

Connor. Her dead husband.

The name feels like my own. But is it? Did I read it in her file? Was it casually looked over as I thumbed through the pages of her life and tossed aside into some dark recess of my mind to later be uncovered?

The file didn't say a damn thing about a dead husband. And it certainly didn't state his name.

The name just came to me.

Do I come clean? Do I tell her I'm a fucking angel-in-training?

"The name just came to me. My memory is blank up until I got my new, um, job. When I thought about the name, I just assumed it was my name," I admit.

She looks skeptical but hasn't slapped me yet. Progress.

"Do you have amnesia or something? Why don't you remember?"

I shrug my shoulders because I can't really tell her.

"Well, before you start claiming my dead husband's name, make sure it's yours to claim first," she snips out.

Then a thought hits me. *Could I be?*

"Well, that's certainly the most bitable ass I've ever seen," Lovenia giggles from the doorway of my room.

Before I can reply, Lark grabs my blanket and tosses it over my ass.

"Show's over, ho," she snaps at Love.

I look over my shoulder to see Lovenia standing in nothing but Omega's white, button-up dress shirt. Her dark nipples are showing through her shirt, and her hair is slightly messy. Looks like they were fucking just as hard as we were.

"Ho? And this comes from the woman with her legs spread open and a man's come running from her. A man she's only known less than a month," Lovenia snarls back.

Lark tenses beneath me.

I peck her on the lips and pull out of her. Sliding next to Lark, I turn my attention toward Lovenia, who smiles sweetly at me and winks.

"What do you want, Love? Don't you need to go keep my best friend warm in his bed?" I question in annoyance. I owe this woman big, but I think busting in on us having sex is a little much.

"Just wanted to tell you one teensy little thing, Al. Remember our conversation last week? If our deal still stands, zip your lips on our 'government' work. I had a feeling you were about to spill the beans to your girlfriend there. Do we still have a deal, mister?"

Fuck you, Lovenia.

I turn my head away from her and look down at my dark angel. My sweet Lark.

"I'm sorry," I whisper to Lark.

She frowns at my words.

"Yes, Love. A deal's a deal."

Lovenia giggles all the way out of my room and down the hallway back to Omega. I groan in frustration.

"I hate her," Lark seethes.

I turn my attention back to the angry woman beside me. "No, you don't." I sigh and peck her on the cheek.

She rolls her eyes, seemingly unconvinced. I drink in her angry features before rubbing my nose against hers. I'll never tire from touching her. Ever. That is exactly my thought as my hand slides up her bare chest, and I touch the cross again.

"Did he give this to you?" I ask as I turn the simple cross over in my fingers.

When her eyes find mine, they mist over. The wound from having lost her family still bleeds profusely and is visible to anyone who takes the time to know her.

"Yes. He gave it to me before he left for his tour of duty," she murmurs.

The hurt in her eyes coupled with the fondness of which she speaks for him twists in my gut. I attempt to force it away, but something ugly curls its way into my heart. As I take a moment to understand what this unfamiliar emotion is, I realize that it's jealousy.

I'm jealous of her dead husband. Jealous of gifts he gave her ages ago. Jealous of the way she still loves him.

I want her to love me.

"Al, we can't be friends or lovers or whatever it is we are," she bursts out suddenly with a rush of air.

The green-eyed monster leaves the building as panic sets in.

"What? Why not?" I demand.

Her pink lips pout out, and my eyes are dragged down to them.

"There are too many secrets. I told you my story, but you won't tell me yours. You say you work for the government, but it's bullshit, Al. If you think I believe that, then you're out of your mind. So, if you think we can be"—she waves between us—"whatever we are, then I suggest you fess up. Your secrets are safe with me."

God, how I want to tell her. All of it. But I can't.

Her green eyes pin me down, and I can't help but defiantly meet her gaze. I will tell her one day. I think. Today's just not that day.

"Lark," I tell her in faux seriousness, "I'm an alien and I've come to snatch your body!"

She furrows her brows in annoyance, but when I begin to tickle her, she squeals with laughter and I'm allowed a temporary reprieve from her damn ultimatums.

"S-stop, y-y-ou a-a-sshole!"

Finally, I stop and admire the way her beautifully colored bare chest heaves from exertion. I want to spend all day worshipping every inch of her breasts with my tongue. From experience, I know she tastes sweeter than any syrup. More delicious than any cake or candy. She tastes like Heaven.

I should know.

"Alpha. The truth."

How the hell am I going to get out of this?

Dipping my lips to her ear, I speak in a whisper. "Trust me that I'll find a way to tell you. Just know there's a big picture here. One you don't understand. Hell, I don't even understand it." I nibble her lobe. "But what I do know is that you and I are here, together. Know that I've given up everything to be with you. Trust me, Twiggy."

She's quiet for a moment but turns her head a bit to give me better access to her ear. The way she writhes uncontrollably against my body sends a thrill of hope through me. I affect her, and as long as I can get my hands on her, she'll always give in.

I need her to give in—*for now.*

With an exaggerated sigh, she mumbles, "I'll try."

Her answer will have to be good enough—*for now.*

Chapter Fourteen

Lark

"I NEED ANOTHER Oreo," Kisha chirps, never taking her eyes from the poem she's working so hard on.

After Alpha and I made love one more time, we rushed to get over here for Poem Day. We were a few minutes late, but Kisha had already taken to bossing the group around and getting them settled. I love that little girl.

"How's your poem coming along?" I question as I squat beside her.

Her page is filled with Ks both lowercase and uppercase. She also drew a rainbow at the top with her pencil.

"It's good, Miss Lark. I'm writing a poem about my favorite things," she tells me as she draws yet another K.

I ruffle her hair before standing.

As I rise, I scan the dirty room. I'd love to have a nice place for these kids. A place with tables and chairs. A place with art boxes filled with crayons and markers. A place with stacks of multicolored paper. I'll keep saving for these kids. One day, I'll give them the sanctuary they deserve.

"Anyone else need a cookie?" I question.

Everyone shakes their heads no, so I allow my eyes to skate over to him.

Alpha.

The man with a weird-ass name who thinks his real one is that of my dead husband.

Connor is a common name.

I ignore the sensible side of me and attempt to douse the tiny internal flame of mine with accelerant.

Alpha has too many secrets.

Alpha knows things about you.

Alpha has ulterior motives.

As if he knows I'm thinking about him, his eyes lift to mine and he grins.

Smiles are the devil.

My knees buckle, and I attempt to blame the sudden weakness on my lack of food. He insisted that we have breakfast before Poem Day, but we'd already wasted too much time on each other's bodies. This morning, when I stepped into their apartment, I had every intention of giving him the what for. I wanted to wring his neck and demand answers. But when I saw the desolate look in his eyes and how lost he appeared to be, I caved.

I wanted to fix him.

Lark doesn't fix people. Hell, she can't even fix herself.

"Are you an angel?" he murmurs with a playful grin.

Damn him and that beautiful smile.

I curl my lip in disgust and roll my eyes at him. "No, I am not an angel."

He chuckles before tacking on his next words. "You look like you fell right from Heaven."

Under normal circumstances, I would flip off someone who was laying on such a cheesy line, but when Alpha says it, it stirs something inside me. Cheesy lines are how I found my husband. Apparently, cheesy lines are my kryptonite.

After the smile that woke me from the darkness of myself, he speaks. The words that come out are awful and adorable all at once.

"Hey, do you have a Band-Aid?" the beautiful man questions.

My eyes frantically scan his body, which appears to be unharmed.

When his blue eyes find mine, they have a mischievous glint to them. I want to put my guard up, but I can't stop looking at his handsome face. The stupid man has me under his spell.

I don't provide him with a verbal answer and shake my head no.

With a smile so big that it reaches all the way from where he is on the sidewalk to my position on the porch steps spreading across his features, he says, "Because I just scraped my knee falling for you."

I blink my eyes several times in shock. Wait. Did he just come on to me?

"Excuse me?" I question. I'm still surprised that the blond-haired man with muscles that barely hide beneath his Marines T-shirt is talking to me. Lark Hutchinson. The girl nobody talks to.

Instead of answering me, he smiles with his eyes trained on me and begins patting himself down. I quirk a brow in question.

"Miss, I seem to have lost my number. Can I have yours?"

Oh.

My.

God.

He really just didn't.

With an eye roll, I stand and turn away from him to go back inside. If I continue to sit here, I'll melt into a puddle of goo on the steps. Lark Hutchinson does not melt. Lark Hutchinson doesn't care about good-looking, cheesy Marines.

"Did you sit in a pile of sugar?" he asks suddenly.

Instinctively, I swipe at my bottom with both hands. Did I sit in something? This is too embarrassing. I need to get away from this man who has just flipped my world upside down with a smile and turn on some Nine Inch Nails or something.

His deep voice is closer when he says his next words. "Because you sure have a sweet ass."

And this is how a Marine steals the heart of a goth queen.

Oorah.

"Work on your poem," I order with a huff.

Alpha grins at me but drops his eyes back down to his paper. I've been running lines in my head, still unsure if I'm ready to share them with anyone yet. Today, I instructed that they write about whatever they want. I'm a little curious as to what he's writing about. He's been hard at work the entire time.

While they write, I think about how poetry became such a big part of my life. In my senior year of high school, I read Edgar Allen Poe's "A Dream Within a Dream." The words—*"is all that we see or seem but a dream within a dream"*—reached right into my soul and unlocked something. This man who wrote the poem seemed to have understood something deep inside me that I couldn't understand myself. After that poem, I became addicted to his work, but also to poetry. I tried my hand at it and found it to be very therapeutic to allow some of the maddening thoughts in my head to escape.

My contemplations are interrupted as the kids begin reading theirs one by one as they finish. I can hardly concentrate on their words because all I can think about is him. Every time I move, every time I glance over at him, his eyes always find me. It's as if his duty in life is to watch my every move. I can't say that I'm disappointed. But I find it wildly distracting to continuously be the center of one's attention.

"Are you okay?" he asks as he stands from his spot on the floor and saunters toward me.

I blink away the daze in my eyes and realize the children are all gone. "I feel a little spaced out," I murmur and absently look around the room.

"You need food, woman. Let's get this stuff picked up and get out of here," he suggests as he gathers the materials.

My eyes follow him and I watch his ass each time he bends over to grab something. His jeans fit his muscular legs well and showcase that firm butt of his. I want to bite it.

A giggle threatens to escape my lips, but I quickly swallow it down. What am I thinking? This sex god before me is a wolf in sheep's clothing. Somehow, I sense that he has motives that, even though they are unknown to me, certainly will affect me. When he brushed off my inquiries, I let him. I fucking let him.

Why?

Why am I bending rules that protect my heart for him? He's not Connor. I know nothing about him. The man just waltzed into my life and I let him right in. I barely put up a fight. Poor Connor had had to work hard for my love. I'd questioned and suspected everything he did until he wore me down one day. With Alpha, he busted through my front door and my walls were immediately down.

It doesn't make sense.

"Ready, Twiggy?" he asks as he approaches me.

I stare dumbly at him and open my bag for him to drop the pens and paper into it. His brows furrow with worry.

Goddamn him and his ability to read me.

"What?" I hiss and attempt to force an annoyed look. I can't manage an annoyed expression, though, because I'm more perplexed than anything. I'm lost inside my head and I can't figure one fucking thing out.

When his concerned, black eyes meet mine, I frown. Then he leans forward and places a soft kiss on my lips, which once again causes me to go all wobbly. Damn him.

"You aren't well, Lark. Let's go to the diner up the street. Hop on. I'm giving you a ride," he instructs.

I bite my lip and try not to smile. I'll never admit how much I enjoy his piggyback rides, but I do. I fucking love wrapping my legs around his strong torso. I love inhaling the delicious, manly smell in his hair. I love the way he protectively grips my thighs when he thinks I'm slipping.

"I can walk," I protest even though I'm already twitching to get my hands on him again.

"Don't make me throw you over my shoulder, woman," he growls.

I mutter out an exaggerated, "Fine," and slide my hands up his back when he turns it toward me. Once I climb on his back, he hands me my bag. I rest my cheek against his shoulder and ignore the many things I should be attempting to figure out like:

What happens at the end of three months?

Who is Alpha with no last name?

What happens when *he breaks my heart?*

The last should be my biggest concern. My fragile pebble of a black heart is all I have left. He has taken it against my will, but once it's gone—when he finally leaves me, because he will—what will be left of me?

I can finally get the hell out of this life and go find my family in the next.

Maybe Alpha is just what I need to hurry up that process.

"Al?" I question with my lips against the soft fabric of his T-shirt.

He glides out of the room and down the stairs as if he floats on air. "Yes, Twiggy?"

I sigh and finally give voice to one of my inner thoughts. "What happens in two months?"

A deep grumble in his chest sends a shiver through me as we burst out of the building and into the warm, LA sunshine.

"Lark, I don't know," he replies with a soft sigh, "but I have two months to figure it out."

Bitch Red is our server again. This time, though, I won't put up with her flirting with him. As she saunters over to us, making it a point to swivel her hips for the good-looking man across from me, I see red—and not the cherry-dyed fake kind.

With a huff of annoyance, I slide out of my seat and loop around the table. Once he realizes that I want to sit with him, he slips an arm around my shoulders and hauls me to him. Being locked in his protective embrace is something I wouldn't mind spending more time doing.

A pop of gum drags me from the heavenly scented bubble that is him.

"Hey, cutie. What can I get you?" she asks pointedly at Alpha, overlooking me altogether.

Irritation crawls its way through my veins like scattering spiders. Unaware of the tension between us, Al spouts off the same order he got the last time we were here—the yogurt parfait included.

As if it's the most annoying thing she's ever had to do, Red turns her attention to me. "What can I get you—Oh my God! Does your shirt really say you hate people?" she demands with red lips forming a shocked "O."

I chuckle darkly. "Yep. You included. Scrambled eggs and orange juice. Oh, and maybe a napkin to clean up your drool from looking at my man."

Her eyes snap to mine and she regards me nastily.

Alpha tightens his hold around me. "That will be all," his authoritative voice booms.

At first, I think he's scolding me, but when I realize he's talking to Red, I internally high-five myself. I watch with glee as she scampers off with her fake-ass red tail between her legs.

Red = 0

Lark = 1

"Your man, huh?" He gives a deep laugh.

I ignore the way it furls its way inside me—twisting and turning and washing over every nerve ending in my body. Instead, I attempt to overlook the way a certain part of my body pulsates eagerly for him, but it's pointless. My body is warm and tense with need to have him again.

"Well, mine for two months, I suppose, Al with no last name."

I expect a retort, but he kisses the top of my head. All I want is to be angry with him—to hate him for making me feel things for him when my heart was given to another long ago. But I can't. Even though I don't fully understand what we are, I do know I don't want him gone.

Ignoring him for the entire week was hell. And after seeing the depression he'd worked himself into—the depression I had caused—I know I don't want to ever ignore him again. I might be a callous, unloving bitch, but I'm not evil.

"I'm going to figure that out," he whispers so quietly that I almost don't hear him.

God, how I want to believe that.

I think.

I don't even fucking know him.

The constant war that wages in my head about Alpha blooms once again to life. He thinks his name is Connor. He showed up out of the blue to rescue me from Pedro. He technically could be deemed a stalker for his obsessively overprotective ways. And he has no job or last name. I don't know the first thing about him, yet I've slept with him several times.

There's just one problem with that argument.

I *feel* like I know him. Something about him invokes in me the same feelings my husband once did long ago. There's a familiarity with Alpha that I felt with Connor. Is it possible to find another person to love in your lifetime? At one time, I would have said no. But now, tucked into Alpha's rock-hard side, I question that answer.

My heart aches at the possibility of loving another like I did my husband. What we had was special and unique. I can't give a part of myself I've already given to Connor to another man. I'll feel as if I'm stealing that part of the *us* we *were* to become the *us* Alpha and I *could be.*

I'll never take that away from the love of my life.

Alpha may be whittling down the rock of my heart to find the inside, but he will never be my husband.

Alpha is not Connor, and I'd be doing myself a favor to remember that.

Lark & Connor = 1

Lark & Alpha with no last name = 0

Chapter Fifteen

Alpha

"READ ME YOUR poem," Lark instructs with a whisper as Red walks away with our empty plates.

I am glad that she ate all of her food and even stole some of my bacon. My Twiggy has an appetite now, and I'm proud to say that she's gained a good couple of pounds while under my watch.

I lift up from my seat and retrieve the folded paper from my back pocket. My gaze is trained on her as she leans back and closes her eyes as if she's looking forward to hearing my poem. The thought of her wanting to hear it warms my heart.

"It's titled, 'Red Hot'," I tease.

Her eyes pop open, and she sticks her tongue out at me. A full-bellied laugh erupts from me, and I see an unwanted smile tease her lips.

Those damn lips.

Leaning over, I press a gentle kiss them. I don't want to pull away, but I do so I can read her the damn poem.

"It's really titled, 'Untitled'," I chuckle.

She swats at me. "Oh my God. On with it already, Al the Poet."

I take a deep breath because this poem, for me, is deep. It doesn't make a lot of sense to me, but it helps to get images and thoughts out of my head and onto paper. It somehow makes them real.

UNTITLED by Al the Poet

Training hard for what's to come.
Dark hair and attitude,
A sudden reprieve from the mindless hum.
Who is she?

Love at first sight,
They say is dumb.
I believe in it though,
Her heart is NOT numb.

Dark, then light, then dark again.
Love, hate, hope, and ~~tears~~ fears.
Souls intertwined, amen.
Blue eyes, headstones, roses, and tears.

Who am I?
Who is she?
Oreos and oorahs,
Light sets her free.

—Alpha

When my eyes find hers again, she's regarding me thoughtfully, tears threatening to spill over.

"I don't know what it means. But I do know it means something," I admit.

Her lips quiver momentarily, but then she purses them together and nods. We both silently regard each other for a short while. I want to know what she thinks about my poem, but I don't dare ask. I can see her mind working in an attempt to figure out what doesn't even make sense to me—and I wrote it.

"Do you have a poem, Lar?" I question as my eyes find her plump lips, which beg to be kissed.

She winces, and I frown in confusion. My words seem to have hurt her.

"Al, please take me home. I should nap before work." Her voice shakes, but she sounds resolved.

Home we shall go.

"I can't fucking believe we're doing this," Omega grumbles beside me.

We're in the building next door to the one we work for headed for a meeting at HEL Enterprises.

Shit. This doesn't feel right.

"Me neither. I'm sorry, O," I groan as we stride toward the only set of elevators in the ornate and expensive lobby.

Over at HEA, they still have the furniture from 1986, it would seem. Here at HEL, they spend their money on luxurious interior decorating.

"You'd do the same for me," he assures me.

He's right, but it doesn't make me feel any better.

When we make it to the elevators, there's one button and it points down. Great.

I mash it and turn to look at my best friend. "So, where's Lovenia?"

"She said she'd meet us there. Where's Lark?"

"Asleep. She has a shift tonight and wanted to nap beforehand. Pedro still alive?"

"For now," he mutters. "But if he keeps eyeing Love, I'm going to have to kick his ass. Last night, he actually licked his lips when she walked by, and it took every ounce of self-control not to pummel his ass."

An uneasy feeling skitters down my spine. He's joking, but I think that, if it came between Love and Pedro, Omega would make the wrong decision. But, considering I've broken every law possible, I have absolutely no room to tell him so.

"What do you think Pallas would say if he knew we were here?" I ask. I hate that I am betraying my boss by not only banging my assignment, but also meeting with Love's boss.

The doors to the elevator finally open and we step inside.

"He'd probably drop that damn cigar right out of his mouth," he laughs. "We're headed to the second-to-the-bottom floor."

I push the button and chuckle with him at the thought of Pallas getting so pissed that he drops his most prized possession. We're still laughing as the doors close. But right before they close all of the way, a hand stops them.

The doors slide back open to reveal a sophisticated man standing on the other side, holding an expensive leather briefcase. His dark hair is slicked back in a stylish way, and his matching goatee is neatly trimmed. When he sees us, his mouth quirks up into a smirk. Omega and I nod our greeting as he steps inside. With the addition of our newest elevator companion, the temperature seems to have risen several degrees in the close quarters.

"Good afternoon, gentlemen." He smiles as he reaches for the button below ours.

Omega and I exchange anxious glances.

"Good day, sir," I return politely.

He extends his hand toward me in greeting. The man is ever a classic fellow with his tweed three-piece suit and manners. I'd imagine him to be much older than Omega and I, except he doesn't look any older than thirty.

Reluctantly, I give his very warm hand a firm shake. Then he releases me and checks the time on his watch before looking my way again.

"Please call me Luc," he instructs jovially. But underneath the jovial front lies something sinister. Something I am not at all comfortable with.

"Luc," I mumble in polite response.

He grins at my words and then turns his gaze to Omega, who is not as trained at hiding his unease as I am. Omega's dark brows are furrowed together and his stance is defensive. He seems ready to pounce.

"What brings you two good boys to our neck of the woods?" Luc inquires on the hot-ass, long-ass journey down.

"We have a meeting," I tell him but don't give him any more details than I have to.

He narrows his dark eyes at me. "Wonderful. With whom?"

"Lovenia and her boss," I reply with hesitation. I'm not at all keen on the way he is probing for information. All we came here to do was have the damn meeting and then get the fuck out.

His eyes light up and he flashes a perfect, white smile at me. "Ahh, sweet Lovenia. She's a favorite of mine."

The way he says her name, with such a lustful tone, sends me on high alert. My eyes flicker to Omega, whose shoulders are now squared and fists are clenched by his sides. Fuck—this is not good. The ride is taking way too damn long and we need out of here before Omega beats the shit out of the obvious head man in charge.

"The woman has some beautiful curves, wouldn't you say?" His question is now directed at Omega, who is not one bit impressed with Luc's seemingly innocent taunts.

"I'd say I'd rather not talk about her with you," Omega growls at him.

Instead of becoming angry, Luc lets out a full-bodied laugh that brings tears to his eyes. Omega and I glance at each other questioningly about the lunatic in the elevator with us.

Luc points a finger at Omega. "I like you, man. I like you a lot."

His comment rubs me the wrong way. This guy should dislike us immensely if we were being good representatives of our company. Instead, he seems rather pleased at our encounter.

"Well, I don't like you," Omega snaps. "And how fucking long is this damn elevator?"

I tense and also ball my fists. If I have to clock my best friend between the eyes to stop an epic showdown from happening, I will. We do not need this guy as an enemy.

"Oh, I *really* like you," he grins back at him, not at all fazed by Omega's temper. In fact, he seems pleased by it.

And that scares the shit out of me.

Omega's curly hair is beginning to kink up due to the stifling heat and the way his sweat is beginning to drench his entire body. I'm sweating like a fucking pig too, but I'm not about to beat the damn boss into the crust of the Earth like he is.

Ding.

Thank fuck.

Our doors open into a dark lobby and I grab Omega's upper arm to haul him out of there.

"Nice meeting you," I throw over my shoulder as we step out.

Luc winks at me as the doors close and he continues his ride down to the bottom floor. Something about his face creeps me the fuck out.

"Dude, did you really have to pick a fight with the devil himself?" I sigh as we make our way down the black, marble floored hallway. The walls are painted black as well to match, and the only light sources are wall sconces every few feet.

"He picked the fight, Al. Not me. I was just going to finish it."

I roll my eyes as we approach the only door on this floor. "And then what?" I question before I turn the knob.

"And then I win."

I twist the warm knob in my fist and smirk at him. "Omega, you are not the baddest motherfucker around. It might do you some good to remember that."

As we walk inside the office, he mutters behind me, "I don't need to be the baddest motherfucker. I just need her."

The both of us are officially fucked.

Chapter Sixteen

Lark

"MARRY ME," HE says with a smile before pressing a kiss on my bare chest.

We're tangled up in the sheets of his bed, and he's told me for the millionth time to marry him. All he has to do is ask, but I won't be told what to do.

"No."

I expect him to climb on top of me and tickle me or playfully nibble on my breast until he pushes inside me and we make sweet love again. What I don't expect is for my fun, adorable, blue-eyed boyfriend to get angry.

I've never seen him get pissed about anything.

He pushes off me and refuses to look at me as he stalks away, naked, toward his bathroom. Tears sting my eyes as I'm suddenly hit with a loss that nearly cripples me. In this exact moment in time, in this tiny corner of the universe, I realize one thing.

I would die if I lost him.

Springing from the bed, I run after him. I can hear the shower running, but once I make it in there, he's standing with both hands on the countertop as he stares in the mirror. His eyes are filled with his own tears, and my heart—what little bit of a heart I have—shatters into a thousand bits.

"I didn't mean it," I sob and throw my arms around his middle.

When I feel his body sag in relief, I really start to cry. How could I have kept pushing him away when all I want is to be with him?

He turns in my arms and kisses me chastely on the top of my head before gripping my shoulders and pushing me away.

Assuming he's done with me, I cry hysterically, but he shushes me before dropping to one knee.

My lovable, naked Connor on one knee, looking at me as if I am his entire world, has to be the most amazing thing I've ever seen—a sight that will always be my favorite.

"Sweet Lark," he murmurs as if it were a prayer, "I love you."

I gasp when he kisses my flesh just below my belly button.

"And I can't live another minute without my last name beside your first name. I can't sleep another night without my ring on your finger. Lar, I can't continue on without knowing that my soul mate is forever committed to me."

My tears haven't stopped, so I can barely see my other half—my Connor. I hear a drawer open and close. When he pushes something onto my ring finger, I cry out with happiness.

"Lark, please marry me. I beg you. I'll spend the rest of my life making sure you're happy. We are meant to be together, and I know without a shadow of a doubt that, when we leave this 'wretched' life you speak of, we'll be holding hands in the next. And the one after that and so on. Make me a happy man and please say yes."

A smile breaks through my tears as I nod in agreement. "Yes, Connor, you lunatic of a man. I'll marry you. You're my forever."

It's not until the next day that he breaks the news about his getting stationed in Afghanistan.

"Please quit."

"It's not that easy."

"What if you don't come back?"

"I will *come back."*

He never comes back.

I wake with a jolt and realize I'm crying. My dreams were nothing but memories. Those dreams are the worst. God, I miss him.

Rolling over, I peek at the clock on my nightstand. It's almost five. Alpha said he'd be back over at six to bring dinner and walk me to work. I'm still upset with him. I don't understand who he is or why he's here. I want to hate it—and him—but I can't. His dark eyes and protective nature draw me in. His warm, delicious body is addicting as hell. But being with him feels like a betrayal to Connor.

My husband.

Tears roll shamelessly down my cheeks as I turn my head to the box in the closet. Suddenly, I need to see his pictures, so I retrieve it once again.

The photo album sits in exactly the same place I left it, and it guts me. All I have left of him is what fits in this box. Long ago, I condensed everything because I couldn't take the constant reminders everywhere. Having it in one simple, small place helped me control the pain.

"I miss you," I whimper as I reach inside and take out the album.

Flipping it open, I let it fall to somewhere in the middle. Two pictures are revealed, and they make me smile through my tears. The first is a selfie Connor took with me when I was asleep, my mouth hanging open while he's kissing my temple. I remember being so pissed that he had taken it because my hair had been a mess and I looked horrible. He told me that I looked like an angel when I slept. I called bullshit but secretly loved his compliment.

"Oh, Connor," I chuckle when I look at the other picture. It's a picture from our honeymoon.

He'd insisted that I bury him in the sand, except for his head, and sculpt a pretend body. Of course I made him a woman with big tits. He couldn't see until afterwards when I showed him the picture. I got tossed into the ocean for that one. His punishment was stealing my bikini bottoms and making love to me in the water with people swimming all around us. It was thrilling and romantic.

A big, fat tear splashes the plastic over the picture, and I quickly swipe it away.

"You promised you'd come back to me, but you lied," I cry and slam the album shut.

As soon as I say the words, I take them back. He'll wait for me after this life. My brain does a mental check of the pill bottles in my medicine cabinet. All it would take is downing the entire bottle of antidepressants and I could probably hurry myself in his direction.

But what about Alpha?

I feel nauseated at the thought of him finding me dead, the man who has been so dead set on protecting me, and I burst into tears. Bile rises in my throat, and I spring from the bed and toward the bathroom. I make it just in time to empty my breakfast into the toilet. As I simultaneously wretch and sob, I want to scream in frustration. Less than a month ago, had I made the decision to end my life, it wouldn't have bothered a soul. But now, with stupid Alpha with no last name, I feel like it would kill him.

I could never hurt him like that.

And that's what makes everything a clusterfuck. He sneaked into my life without any regard as to what it would do to my head. I'd been plugging along day by day and managed to carve out a simple life for myself that didn't include people, aside from my little Poem Day kids, or emotions. It certainly wasn't a life where any love was allowed.

Yet here I am on the cold tile floor of my bathroom, puking my guts up and missing the mysterious man from across the hallway.

God, you have to help me through this one.

A shiver courses through me, but I feel a bit better after having vomited. I shakily stand and flush the toilet. Once I've brushed my teeth, I briefly wish my mother were here. She was always good at taking care of her only child when she'd get sick. When I lost my family, she tried her best to take care of me. I was hopeless.

I could call her . . .

I want to cry at the thought of her familiar hand stroking my hair. I hate to admit it, but I miss her. Damn Alpha and his fucking with my head. If she were here, she'd make me some chicken and dumplings, her specialty, and bring me ginger ale.

After finding some insane nerve within me, I decide to do something rash. Quickly, before I lose the fire, I run over to my purse and pull out my phone. She doesn't have this number, but I know the house number by heart.

"Hello?" her sweet, feminine voice answers on the second ring.

A ragged sob rushes from me, and I hear her gasp on the other line.

"Baby, is that you?" I can hear the quivering of her voice.

I can't form words. Only tears.

"Shh, honey. I'm here. Where are you living these days? I could come to you," she whispers in a hope-filled tone.

I shudder violently but manage to find my voice. "I'm so sorry."

"Oh, Lark. Please let me see you," she begs.

She can't see me shaking my head, but there's no way I can see her right now.

"Please," she tries again before her voice gives away to hysterical sobs.

"I love you," I tell her between hiccups.

"I know you do, baby. I love you too."

"Goodbye, Mom," I rush out before mashing the button to end the call.

She must call fifteen times before finally giving up. After several times of watching the phone ring and letting it go to voicemail, I see a text finally comes through.

Unknown number: Please let me see you.

For the first time in a long time, I want to see her too.

Me: Soon. I promise.

As I watch him saunter across the room in nothing but a towel, my mouth waters. I've made love to him hundreds of times, but the sight of his body never grows old. He's one hundred percent man, and I love touching and tasting every inch of him.

"You know"—he quirks up a brow in a teasing manner—"now that you're officially my wife, you have certain 'duties'."

I burst out laughing when he does a pelvic thrust at me.

"Is that so, babe? And what do these 'duties' entail?" I tease back.

Today, our wedding was small and simple. It was perfect. Now, we can begin our life together, and we plan on starting with consummating our marriage.

"Well . . ." He grins evilly as he drops his towel. "You have to let me knock you up. Those curvy hips of yours were made to carry babies."

I scoff at him and flip him the bird. "I don't remember the preacher mentioning anything about, 'Thou shalt knock up thy wife immediately'."

He grins and climbs onto the bed. I can see how ready he is to make said babies by the bounce of his very hard, very impressive cock.

"He told me in private. Guy stuff. Oh, and he said you have to give me a blow job at least every other day."

I sit up on my knees and challenge him with a glare. Of course he's onto me by now and knows that my glares mean shit because I'm powerless against his adorable self. When I slide a hand around his cock, though, he groans. He's powerless when it comes to me as well, so we're evenly matched.

"What if I want to break the rules and give them to you every day?" I purr seductively and lick my lips for good measure.

"Goddammit, woman," he growls and smashes his mouth against mine.

I stroke him while he kisses me as if his life depends on it. When I moan against his lips, he slips a hand under my ass and flops me onto my back. I spread my legs around his hips and eagerly wait for him to enter me. But instead of slamming right into me like we both want, he pauses and breaks our kiss.

"What are you waiting for, husband? Mark me. I'm your wife now, so claim me," I taunt.

The hunger in his eyes turns his blue eyes a dark shade of navy. They're almost black.

"Sweet Lark, you're mine forever. Understand? No matter what happens, you're always mine. Promise me."

"Yes, Connor, I promise. Now make love to me already!"

This time, he does slam into me.

This time, our souls do mate.

This time, he seals our love with the connection of our bodies.

"Mine," he reminds me as he thrusts hard into me.

With each slap of our flesh, I feel his claiming promise over and over again.

Growing up, I never imagined myself to be a woman that would let a man claim her. But this isn't just any man. This is Connor. He's different. He's mine also.

"Connor," I gasp as he pumps into me.

"What, baby?"

"Promise me something too."

"I'll promise you whatever you want. You know that," he murmurs before sucking on my bottom lip.

"Yes, but I need to hear it. Promise me that, when we leave this life, you'll find me." Tears well in my eyes as we make love, but I need to hear these words from him. I need him to promise me that, when this short lifetime is over, we'll still be together.

"Lar, I will find you. Nothing will stop me, you death-obsessed woman."

I believe him. I truly do.

I just don't expect him to leave his lifetime so soon—and without me.

I step out of the shower and let the memory swirl down the drain with the water. Why am I suddenly being flooded with memories of Connor? Guilt curls its way into my gut, and I feel sick again. I made a promise to him, yet here I am with Alpha. This can't go on.

As I towel off, I straighten my back and find my resolve. I love Connor. Still. And I'll be damned if I let anyone get in my way of finding him again.

Sorry, Alpha, but the dead husband just trumped you.

Chapter Seventeen

Alpha

I PUSH THE door to the office open and can't help but drink in the beauty. For a windowless office, it seems airy and light, unlike the dark hallway. The walls are painted cream, and everything looks soft—even the two demons sitting at the conference table beside the huge, glass desk.

"Omega! Alpha!" Lovenia chirps as she bounces from her chair. Today, she's wearing a demure, white, knee-length dress. Her normally sultry dark waves have been twisted up and pinned to her head. If I didn't know any better, I'd say she looked angelic.

Too bad I know better.

Before I can give Omega a look that says, *Be cool,* he pulls her into his arms and kisses her with a soft peck on her lips. So not cool. I can already tell that this meeting is not going to end well.

"Hello, gentlemen," a deep voice says from behind Lovenia. "I'm Corson."

Since Omega is still lip-locked with Love, I extend my hand in greeting. These demons are all so off-putting with their good looks and seemingly innocent faces. Corson isn't any different than Luc or Lovenia. He has short, brown hair that's been gelled in a stylish but not greasy way, pale-blue eyes, and a grin that probably serves him well with the ladies. His perfectly expensive suit matches his eyes, and I wonder if he planned it that way.

"Please have a seat. Lovenia speaks so highly of the both of you," he smiles as he waves his hand toward the table.

Love and Omega finally break their kiss but hold hands as they walk over to take their seats. Once we all sit, Omega and I both fix our gazes on Corson.

"So Lovenia tells me you two are something pretty special over at HEA." He winks at her.

She nods emphatically as if she's proud, but I know the truth. Omega's features darken as he watches Corson's eyes drop down to the cleavage of the dress I'm realizing is not so innocent anymore. I try to warn Omega with my eyes that they're playing some sort of wicked game, but he won't even look at me. He's too busy clenching his jaw and appearing ready to rip this man's head off.

"We're just two guys trying to make something for ourselves. Everyone wants to be happy," I respond.

The tension from Omega's end is thick. Lovenia seems pleased as fucking punch with herself. And Corson . . . I don't know what to think about him yet.

"Ahh, happiness. I bet you two would do just about anything for happiness—or is it *love* that you'd put everything on the line for?" His question is directed to me.

Omega sits up in his chair because Corson put emphasis on the word "love" and, like a jackass, he's reading it as *Love*nia.

I nod but don't speak. I'm not sure what this guy wants from us, so I'm certainly not going to give him any more information than I have to. I'm here because Lovenia promised to keep my secret from Pallas and everyone over at HEA. This is my end of the bargain. Other than that, he can kiss my ass.

"Maybe you already have," Corson ponders aloud.

My gaze swoops over to Lovenia, and she smiles sheepishly at me.

"Shit happens," I growl to Corson while still holding Lovenia's stare.

The demons chuckle at my sudden anger—as if they were expecting and are pleased with my reaction.

"Can we cut to the fucking chase?" Omega snarls. "I need to get back to my assignment."

I think about Lark, who is sleeping before her shift. I wanted to curl up behind her and hold her, but instead, I'm here. With these two bozos. Talking in fucking circles.

"Yes, Omega. We can cut to the *fucking* chase. Here's the deal. I've heard a lot about you. Not just from the beautiful and alluring Lovenia." Corson pauses to wait for the possessive reaction of Omega—which he gets, of course, in the form of a growl. "But also from word on the street. Reapers and Leviathans all know who the dynamic duo over at HEA is. Those angels can't stop talking about you, either. And Pallas? He's proud as can be of you two."

His grin is pure evil, and I instantly put my guard up.

"In fact," he continues, "when Pallas and I met up today in the cigar lounge, he told me you both were doing so well on your final assignment. He'd even jumped the gun a bit and put in the order for your wings."

My wings. All I ever wanted was my wings. And Lark gave them to me . . .

"Pallas knows better to jump the gun on anything. Even for us," Omega snaps.

He's right though. I think we can both sniff out a lie.

"Even if he did," I drawl out, "what does it matter to you? To Lovenia? We have our jobs to do, and you have yours."

Corson nods and places his elbows on the table. Then he steeples his fingers together as if he's contemplating his next strategic move in a game. We're probably pawns in this dumbass's game.

"That we do, Alpha," he agrees. "Which is why I want to present to you an offer."

Omega stands so suddenly that the chair behind him falls to the thick carpet with a thud. "We don't make deals with the devil."

Corson and Lovenia burst out laughing as if he'd said the funniest fucking thing ever. I rise from my chair, indicating that this meeting is over.

"Please, gentlemen. Sit. I wasn't trying to offend you. Just hear what I have to say."

Omega rolls his eyes and picks up the chair but doesn't sit. I take his cue of distrust and stand behind my chair as well. We haven't left, but we're defiant enough to not sit down and let him play us on his invisible fucking strings.

"Fine. Stand there. But listen. You"—he points to Omega—"want something I have." Corson's eyes flicker over to Lovenia, who bats her eyelashes at him.

I expect Omega to laugh in his face or flip him off. What I don't expect is for him to fold his arms across his thick chest and nod in agreement.

Fuck.

"And you"—he now points at me—"have fallen in love with your assignment. Am I right?"

My jaw clenches, but I give him a curt nod.

We're so fucked.

"Good thing for you two gentlemen, I can help. What if I told you that you could have what you want? Would that interest you?"

Omega and I remain stone-faced—neither of us answering his question though I know both of us are considering his words.

"Just think it over. Why should you have to have a career *or* love? Why can't it be both? Here at HEL Enterprises, we pay handsomely and we believe in our employees getting what they want. There's no reason to deny our employees of anything. We're low on Leviathans and could use a couple of tough motherfuckers like the both of you. You wouldn't have to be some lowlife Reaper to prove yourself first. We're offering you a position at the rank of sweet Lovenia here. It's an offer you can hardly refuse."

Omega glances at me, and for the first time in the six years I've known him, I see the hesitation to do what's right for the sake of what he wants. Can I blame him? I'm quite tempted myself just to be with Lark.

But we can't. There have to be more strings attached to this deal.

"We'll think about it," Omega blurts out, which earns him a death glare from me.

"Wonderful. That was exactly the answer I was hoping for. Keep thinking, gentlemen. I mean, who wouldn't want a nine-to-five job with more benefits than you could imagine. A job that starts out with more seniority that you'll have even as Seraph Guardians, which, by the way, are twenty-four-hours-a-day, seven-day-a-week jobs. Wouldn't it be nice to have time off to spend time with the one you love? The offer stands for one week. I'll expect an answer one way or the other by next Sunday."

Corson and Lovenia stand from their seats, and she walks over to plant a kiss on Omega's cheek. Instinctively, his arm snakes in an over-protective manner around her waist.

We're definitely fucked.

"What happens if we say no?" I question.

The demon's pale eyes darken. "Then it looks like you're in a whole lot of deep shit over at HEA. I have my dear friend Pallas on speed dial."

Fuck this asshole. Now, I don't have two months to figure this shit out. I have one damn week.

The only answer that matters is Lark.

I knock hard on her door for the fifth time. As soon as we left HEL, Lovenia and Omega went over to Pedro's. Omega was tight-lipped and acting somber, but I could see the decision forming behind his eyes. He and I are going to need a serious sit-down talk without Lovenia's influence.

If I have to knock a sixth time, I'm going to bust the fucking door open. Thankfully, I hear the flip of the deadbolt and her door is spared.

I turn the knob and push through to see Lark twisting her long, wet hair into a messy bun.

"What?" she asks as she pulls a bobby pin from between her lips and pulls back a loose strand of hair.

"You're beautiful and I missed you," I tell her simply as I shut the door behind me and lock it.

"I didn't miss you," she snips out without making eye contact with me.

Something's off. The woman I left earlier today is not the woman standing before me. Something happened while I was gone.

"Are you okay?" I question. I want to kiss the hell out of her, but I don't move. It would be like chasing after a scared kitten. Rushing her will only make her run. And the look in Lark's eyes right now says that she'll most definitely run, which isn't what I want at all.

"No, Al, I am not okay. Okay? I had dreams about my husband. The man I *do* love," she bursts out as tears well in her eyes.

Her comment cuts me deep, but I remain strong for her.

"What about me?" My words blurt out before I can stop them.

Green eyes meet mine, and her lip quivers. When I take a step toward her, she takes one step back.

"What about you?" she retorts as a tear runs down her cheek.

Another cut to my soul.

"He's gone, and I love you now," I murmur as prowl toward her.

This time, she doesn't move. "Alpha, I promised him. Being with you breaks that promise. Besides, I don't even know you." She just keeps cutting me with her words.

After another stride closer, I'm within reaching distance of her. Her chest, which I know is bare underneath her dress, heaves wildly.

"He's dead, baby. You have me now."

Another tear chases the last one down her cheek. I reach up and swipe it away with my thumb. With a whimper, she leans slightly toward it, giving me hope. Sliding my hand into her hair, I take the last step until our chests touch.

"I can't," she tells me with a shaky voice but doesn't move away.

I don't believe her words because she doesn't believe them. We both can hear the uncertainty in her voice.

"I love you, Lar," I whisper, bringing my lips close to hers.

"You can't love me so soon, you insane man."

I chuckle against her lips, and she shivers.

"Insane for you, baby."

She bursts into hysterical giggles that make her seem like she's the more insane one than I. "I hate cheesy lines." I'm not at all convinced.

I raise a brow at her and grin. My hands skim down to her waist before I pull her tighter against me. "If I were a cat, I'd spend all nine lives on you. I bet you really hated that line." I smile and waggle my eyebrows.

She caves. Thank fuck she caves.

"I tried to be strong, Al," she whimpers as I nibble her lips.

She tastes like a hint of toothpaste, and I want more. When she parts her mouth, I deepen our kiss and really savor her.

"You are strong," I assure her between heated kisses.

Her small hands run up my chest and into my hair. I'm entranced by the way she tugs me closer and tangles her tongue with mine.

"Not strong enough. I failed him," she moans when I tear my mouth from hers to trail kisses along her cheek, to her jaw, and finally to her neck.

"But you didn't fail me. You love me too, Twiggy, even if you won't admit it."

And she doesn't admit it, but I still believe it as truth.

Chapter Eighteen

Lark

I'M POWERLESS AGAINST him. Just like I used to be with Connor. Is it possible to love two people in your lifetime? What happens when this lifetime is over? Who do you choose in the afterlife?

"You're mine, Lar," Alpha breathes against my neck as if he's answering my unspoken questions. I squirm when he sucks the flesh into his mouth and gently bites it.

When one of his hands cups one of my breasts, I let out another embarrassing moan before saying, "He said the same thing, Al. Don't you see why I'm hurting?" Then I cry out as he pinches my nipple through my dress.

"Fuck him. You're mine. I've been to Hell and back for you. I won't lose you," he growls.

I don't want to lose him. But what about . . .

His hands glide down my body and push my dress up. I gasp when he takes the fabric of my skimpy panties and rips them right from my body.

"What are you doing?" I breathe out as his large hands palm my ass as he hauls me closer to him.

"Climb on, Twiggy. I'm about to take you for a ride," he croons.

I jump without hesitation as he lifts me and then hook my ankles around his hard ass. He strides over to the closest wall—the front door to be exact—and pushes my back against it. I hold on to his neck while he makes quick work of unbuckling his jeans and rids them down along with his boxers.

Claim me. I'm yours.

He enters me so hard and fast that I swear the door cracks from the impact. I yelp out his name as he slams into me over and over. With each thrust, I feel him marking my soul as his, and selfishly, I let him. I may miss my husband with every ounce of my being, but Alpha owns a part of me too—the greedy part of me that says that I can have both, that I don't *have* to choose.

"You love me," he groans as he pushes as deep as he can into me.

I don't answer him. I can't give him the words, but he knows.

"What happens when we die?" I ask suddenly as I feel my body begin to tingle from the pleasure of an impending orgasm.

His black eyes find mine, and for a moment, they're so light that they almost seem midnight blue. "What happens if we live instead?"

My eyes flutter closed as his words attach themselves to my very being. They thread their way through my soul, and I wonder.

"What happens if we live instead?"

A shudder rips through my body as I lose myself to my climax. Tears roll out as I realize I've completely lost myself to this man. To the man whose last name I don't even know. I feel him tense up before a burst of heat shoots deep into me. My pussy hugs his cock over and over as if it's thanking him for his love.

We stay wrapped up in each other and still attached, but he pulls away enough to look at me. With the way his eyes roam over every curve of my skin so reverently, I feel as if I'm his everything.

"Who are you?" My mind-plaguing questions slips out.

He groans in frustration, and I see the indecision in his eyes. I can see that he wants to tell me exactly who he is, but something stops him. Lovenia and his "government" works stop him. It's confusing as hell, but whatever it is scares him from coming clean.

"I'm yours. Just Al."

I sigh but lean forward, searching for his lips. "What if I want more than Just Al?"

"You have all of me, Lar. All. Of. Me. Everything I do now is for you and because of you. Don't you get that? You're my life and my forever."

Forever.

I wince at the word. Connor thought that I was his forever, too, and look how that ended up.

As Alpha's lips brush against mine, I'm dragged right back to him. When I'm with this man, he's all I can think about. And as upsetting as it is to forget my dead husband in the process, I can't help but love the power he has over me. I've only felt this way one time before, with one other person. It saved me from myself then—just like it is now.

"Lark, you're a good person." He whispers it so softly that I almost mishear his words. Then he thickens within me and slowly peels me away from the door.

I hold on as he saunters—with me attached to him—into my bedroom and kicks out of his jeans and shoes along the way.

"Why do you say that as if it surprises you?" I question when he reaches my bed.

His hand finds the bottom of my dress and pulls it up over my head, leaving me in nothing but my boots and cross necklace. While I wait for him to answer, I help him out of his shirt.

"I had you pegged for a bad girl. But you're not. They were wrong."

"*They were wrong.*"

"Who was wrong?"

Instead of answering me, he lowers us onto the bed without ever detaching himself from me and slowly thrusts his hips against me. A moan echoes in the room, and I bite my lip when I realize that it was mine.

"You're an angel, Lar. My angel."

I close my eyes as he makes love to me. I'm his angel.

"You're my angel," Connor breathes against my lips.

"Connor, I'm hardly an angel.

"I love you, Twiggy," Alpha whispers against my neck.

"I love you, my death-obsessed wife."

Tears.

Tears.

My brain flops back and forth from past to present, nearly giving me whiplash.

"I love you too, army boy."

"Marines. Oorah."

"Alpha," I cry out as he pushes my thigh against my belly and takes me deeper than he ever has before.

"Stay with me, baby," he utters as if he knows my mind is all over the place.

"What am I doing?" I sob but then gasp as pleasure sears through every nerve ending in my body, causing me to buck beneath him.

"Lark, you're living."

I snap my eyes open and flip my head to the side. "Shit. I'm late." The clock reads twenty-three after seven.

"Call in. Stay here with me. In bed," Alpha pleads. The desperate tone in his voice makes me consider his request, but I already let Gus down enough.

"Ugh, don't tempt me. Get dressed and make me some food, good-lookin'," I tease as I roll out of bed and begin throwing on my clothes.

Given a new mission—food always gets him—he bounds from the bed and dresses quickly. I swiftly touch up what little makeup I'm wearing and put on a new pair of panties before heading out of my room to find him. I hear the microwave ding as I round the corner.

"What's for dinner?" I question.

He smiles sheepishly at me as he pulls a Hot Pocket out of the microwave and then hands it to me. Luckily for him, he's cute. I get damn tired of eating these things.

I feel bad when he doesn't make one for himself but instead hunts my purse down for me.

"You aren't going to eat?"

"I'll have dessert later." His wink that follows is suggestive.

I roll my eyes and take my purse as we leave my apartment. "You're a pig," I laugh as he locks my door.

When he turns to me, I lift onto my toes and kiss his cheek. His gaze drifts beyond me to down the hallway, and a growl so fierce tears from his chest, scaring the shit out of me.

"What?" I hiss and whirl around, assuming Pedro is after me. But when I look down our decrepit hallway, all I see is closed doors. No people. His gaze is trained on the stairwell, and the glower in his eyes is so incredibly hate-filled that it sends a tremor of terror down my spine.

The moment lasts for several seconds before Alpha finally relaxes and turns a worried stare toward me. His palms find my neck, and he crashes his lips to mine. I melt in his confusing kiss. The kiss seems protective and apologetic—relieved even.

What the fuck just happened?

"Alpha?"

"I won't let anyone hurt you. There's only one place you're destined to go and it's in my arms," he assures me cryptically.

His anxious tone freaks me the fuck out. Is the government after me? Does this have something to do with Connor? Was he in some sort of trouble before he died, and now, I'm being sought after?

The questions don't stop and my mind whirls around and around as Alpha escorts me down the stairs and out of the building. Tonight, the LA air is sticky and I'm thankful for the dress I'm wearing. Alpha's guard is still up, though, because his eyes dart all over the place as if every shadow we pass is a threat.

I don't push him for any more answers as we make our way to Gus's tattoo shop. Honestly, I am slightly afraid of what the answers will be. Nothing makes sense in this world, but ignorance is bliss, they say. My thoughts are chased away as we approach the stairs. Gus is pacing the top of the landing and nerves threaten to have the dinner I inhaled on our walk make a reappearance.

"Dammit, Lark. Where the fuck have you been?" he snarls when he sees me.

Alpha tenses beside me, and I physically have to pull him to me. "Don't talk to her that way unless you want to meet every step with your ugly-ass teeth!"

I snap my head over to see my overprotective man glaring up at Gus. "Sorry, Gus. And, Al, cool it," I warn as I hop up the steps.

"Your client has been waiting for forty-five minutes and he looks rich. You're making me look bad, Lark. This may be just a job for you, but it is my business. Now get in there and take care of him. Please," he grumbles.

I sigh and nod that I will. Alpha is hot on my heels and must give big, badass Gus a look that has him shitting his pants, because he actually cowers under his glare.

Normally, Al would leave me to work and do whatever he does, but not tonight. Tonight, he follows me right into the parlor as if threats are everywhere. I shake my head in annoyance as I storm over to my station. A man in a navy, tweed, three-piece suit is leaning against the wall near my doorway.

"I'm so sorry," I apologize as I approach the dangerously good-looking man. My heart might be tied up with Alpha's, but I'm still a woman and can appreciate a fine specimen of a man. And my client is just that—hot.

"No need to be sorry, lovely," he grins. He seems unaffected by my tardiness, completely opposite from what I was expecting according to Gus's reaction.

"Why are you here?" Alpha blurts rudely.

I twist my head toward him and fire off a warning glare.

The man smiles at Alpha in a friendly manner, as if his rudeness doesn't affect him. "So nice to see you so soon, Alpha. I'm here to get a tattoo. I hear she's wicked at what she does."

For some reason, I blush at his compliment, but Alpha seems ready to explode. How do these two know each other?

"She's not wicked at anything, so back the fuck off," he snarls back.

The man frowns but only for a moment. I feel as if I'm going to suffocate from the heat of their standoff. The food from earlier grumbles in my belly, and I feel ill.

"Al, chill the hell out or I'll have Gus escort you out of here," I threaten.

He doesn't seem at all worried about my threat, but he does zip his lips.

"What'll it be today, sir?" I question as I drop my purse in the corner and begin washing my hands.

"Please call me Luc."

Out of the corner of my eye, I see the client now known as Luc begin to unbutton his suit jacket. As I prep my area, I hear him removing the necessary clothing and drapes them on a waiting chair. When I finally turn back to him, he is naked from the waist up. His contoured body, much like Alpha's, is also a blank slate. Unlike Al, though, his skin is slightly fairer.

"What do you want?" I ask him as I attempt to peel my eyes away from the skin that is as blank as paper. Skin I am itching to ink up.

"I want *you*"—he pauses dramatically, which draws out a huff from Alpha—"to tattoo a cross on my chest. I was going to have you do wings on my back, but that is kind of tacky, don't you think?"

Alpha mutters a string of curse words under his breath, and I bristle at Luc's underhanded comeback.

"Wings are sexy—especially mine," I snap. "Now lie down on your back and I'll give you what you want."

Luc flashes me what he must think is a hot grin—and to most women, it probably is—but I think it seems disgusting and arrogant. "Darling, the cross I want is special though. I want to be able to look down and see it. I'm also a big fan of snakes. A thick, green-eyed serpent twisting around it would be quite exquisite, don't you think?"

The vision he creates with his words sends my mind into a frenzy as I paint his skin with my eyes.

"So, you want an upside-down cross, essentially? You're weird. Lie down," I order.

He chuckles but does as he was told. I slip my gloves on and drag my rolling table over to the bed. My clients are used to me climbing all over them to get in the perfect position to ink them, and Luc is no different. Although Alpha is going to hate it.

"Al, I'm feeling kind of hot. Do you think you could get me a cold drink? Maybe a few Oreos?"

His eyes widen, but he must see the paleness of my skin. With a grunt, he chooses to help me instead of protect me like I'm his cavewoman. Once he's gone and after I've quickly sketched out a rough image of what Luc described, I grab my gun and straddle my client. His body is incredibly warm, and I'm glad Al went after something for me to drink. This will be a long night, otherwise.

Luc's lips curl into a naughty grin as I rub the skin with my gloved hand. My mind analyzes the size and colors that will make this design perfect. Unfortunately, my customer must have analyzed the way my legs feel wrapped around him, because I feel him harden beneath me.

I raise a brow and pin him with a glare. "You better knock that out right now, buddy. My boyfriend will kick your ass. You've been warned."

He full-belly laughs at my words as if I'm a cute puppy nipping at him. "I think you'd be worth an ass-kicking."

I ignore his flirting and begin my art. I've barely started my design when I hear Alpha come back. He sets a glass of ice water and the cookies on my table without interrupting me. Then he kisses my head but doesn't say anything. I also realize for a fleeting moment that he remains nearby, within touching distance.

The cross is large. The longer of the too planks—for some reason, a weathered, wooden cross came to my mind—starts between his clavicle and with elegant smooth lines shoots out down toward his rippled abs. The other plank intersects just below his pecks and is shorter. I must spend hours on the details of the cross alone, occasionally sipping my water. When it's empty, I absently see that Al has refilled it.

When I begin working on the serpent, my client finally speaks.

"I want her to have eyes the same color as yours."

The serpent is a *her* and she will have emerald-colored eyes like mine.

Creepy.

I have the weirdest customers.

Chapter Nineteen

Alpha

I SHOULD KILL him. If I thought I actually could, I would. But I'm not stupid. Hotheaded at times, yes, but not stupid. I'm not Omega, for crying out loud.

Lark is seemingly oblivious to the darkness she's straddling so innocently. But I'm watching him. I watch every twitch of his muscles. Every lust-laden glance he sends her way. The way he clutches her thigh when the pain becomes unbearable. If I were a normal man watching another man touching my woman, I'd have no qualms about knocking him on his ass.

Luc is no normal man though, and neither am I.

Luc and I work on opposite ends of the spectrum. Unfortunately, he's not someone to be messed with, and he is far more powerful than I am. My best bet is to only make a move if I have to. And I will if I have to. But right now, I'll wait his ass out.

As Lark leans close to his chest to work out some of the details of the serpent's mouth, I get a glimpse of her bare breasts, which means that motherfucker can see them too. I'm about to distract her so she'll end his show, but I don't have to. The cross around her neck slides out of her dress and lands on his chest.

Then all Hell breaks loose.

"Fucking bitch!" Luc roars in agony as he grabs her shoulders and pushes her away from him.

I'm about to kill him, but she thinks he's just being a pussy from the needle, so I keep my clenched fists at my side.

"Stop being a goddamned baby, Luc," she snaps and pushes him back down onto the bed.

I step closer to her and get a glimpse of his face. His eyes watch in horror as her cross swings toward him every time she leans forward with her gun. It doesn't touch him, but he squirms each time. I find satisfaction in watching the fear in his eyes. Power thrills through my veins from knowing that it bothers him. I lock the information away in my head for a later time.

"There. You're done." She smiles as she lifts up.

I can tell she's dizzy now that she's rejoined reality by the slight sway of her body. She's been in the same position for hours, and I need to get her home. Rushing over to her, I hook an arm around her waist and pull her away from the darkness and into my light. It almost seems as if she's drawn into some unseen magnetism of mine because she allows me to sweep her into my arms and hold her tight.

"Your work is beautiful, Twiggy," I tell her and then kiss the top of her head. I remember how upset she was when I failed to praise her last time.

Her arms snake around my waist and she squeezes me. "Thanks, Just Al."

I flick my gaze over to Luc and see him looking down at the tattoo in appreciation. Pride swells in my chest because Luc may be the baddest of them all, but at the end of the day, even he is in awe of her talent. She's a star.

Luc struts over to his clothes and pulls his dress shirt on but leaves it open to air out his raw chest. Then he removes a business card from his pocket and extends his long arm toward her. My girl is too smart for her own good, because she doesn't reach for it.

"What's that?" she asks as if he's holding a snake.

While waiting for him to answer, she quickly sets to dressing his tattoo before he leaves.

"A business card, sweetheart. You're quite the artist. I run a company full of people who appreciate art like yours. We could always use someone full time like you on staff. I pay very, *very* well." He flashes a wicked grin.

I hiss out a breath of air when she takes the simple, black card from him.

"Wow, Luc. A job offer from the Devil himself. Pass." She smirks and tosses the card onto her side table.

I have the urge to laugh at him, but he's not at all impressed by her rejection.

"Don't be so quick to reject my offer, darling. Your dear *boyfriend* here was just at my office this afternoon entertaining an offer of his own. How nice would it be for you to spend all of that time together but be paid more than you could probably ever spend?" he says smoothly.

When she cuts her eyes over to mine, I know I'm in trouble for not having told her about my meeting.

"Unless you'd like more tattoos, I suggest you run along, sir," she snarls, disgusted.

He picks up his jacket and tie and then pulls out a wad of cash. With a grin, he tosses the money onto the table beside his card. "There's a tip in there for you."

She mutters her thanks but nonverbally dismisses him when she sets to cleaning her tools. I, on the other hand, keep my eyes on the sharp-dressed demon. He watches her with a longing look for several moments before winking at me. I suppress the growl that thrashes to leave my throat. I'm so close to throttling this motherfucker. As if he knows I'm about to snap, he flashes me a sly grin before he turns on his heel and strides out of the parlor.

It isn't until he's long left the building that the temperature falls a few degrees and I can breathe a sigh of relief.

"What an arrogant prick," she mutters as she finishes up. "Why did you go to see him?"

Her question catches me off guard, but I attempt to answer her as honestly as I can.

"I owed Lovenia a favor. She wanted me and Ome—*Omar* to meet her boss. We ran into that guy in the elevator. I thought Omar was going to kick his ass then, and I was afraid I was going to have to kick his ass tonight. Anyway, we won't be taking them up on their offer because they're bad . . . *businessmen.*"

She searches my eyes for lies but finally nods her head in satisfaction. With a ragged breath of relief, I bend and retrieve her purse.

"I don't like him." She's blunt about her feelings toward him as she snaps the light off.

Sliding my arm around her, I pull her to me and kiss the top of her head. "I don't like him, either. Now, let's get you home so I can have my dessert."

The entire way back to the apartment is spent playfully flirting, and I love the fact that she lightened up after Luc left. If I could freeze the mood she's in and let her live in it forever, I would. No sadness. No anger. Only the two of us laughing and touching—how it should be.

"Climb on, Twiggy. Time for a ride," I tell her when we get to the stairs.

She giggles—which is music to my fucking ears—and slides her palms up my back to my neck. I bounce extra hard on each step, causing her to squeal and my booming laughter to echo in the stairwell. When we reach the top of the stairs, though, the laughter dies in my throat.

A Reaper.

Same fucker as before.

When we left Lark's apartment earlier, I saw this asshole prowling around in our hallway. Either way, he's not getting Pedro or Lark. It's too fucking soon.

His dull, red eyes find mine, and he grins a toothy grin at me. All Reapers are the same. They wear all black and look like greasy-ass weasels. They're the lowest on the totem pole at HEL, and they may as well be shit on my shoe as far as I'm concerned. I'm used to dealing with them as a Minder, but they come when the assigned time says that they'll come. Never earlier.

So why in the fuck is this fucker here? Two months early?

Thank fuck Lark can't see him. Reapers aren't visible to humans. And even though Omega and I are in human form, there are some powers that haven't been fully taken from us. Seeing their kind and our kind is one of those powers. We need that power in order to do our job properly.

My glare is menacing as I warn him to leave us the fuck alone. With a smirk, he simply folds his arms across his chest. It makes me want to wring his neck and beat the hell out of him, but Lark will think I've lost my mind. Instead, I prowl past him without taking my eyes from him. Before I make it to Lark's door, I bang on ours.

"What are we doing?" she asks.

"I just need to tell Omar something," I say, attempting to reassure her.

"Hmph."

Damn, her ability to sniff out lies is annoying.

The door swings open to Omega's smug grin. He's only wearing a towel around his waist, and his hair is a wet mop.

"What's up, brother?"

"Maybe you should be a friendly *neighbor* and check on your *friend*," I warn him.

His gaze falls beyond me, and when he sees the Reaper, his back straightens. "Motherfucker," he grumbles and pushes past me into the hallway.

The Reaper chuckles darkly but disappears down the stairs.

Lark observes our unusual exchange but doesn't say a word. I have a feeling I'll get grilled once inside her apartment.

"I'm on it, buddy," he assures me.

I nod and stride over to Lark's apartment. Once I set her down, she fishes her keys from her bag and then hands them to me. I unlock the door and toss a glance down the hallway while she steps inside. The asshole is gone, but that doesn't mean I'll drop my guard. He's two months early and that scares the fuck out of me. I want to hope that he's here for Pedro, but that means Omega would be in deep shit.

And if he's here for Lark . . .

I can't even finish that thought. Following her in, I shut the door and throw the deadbolt in place.

"Al."

I groan because I know what she wants. Turning to her, I shrug my shoulders. "Just a hunch?"

She tosses her purse on the kitchen table. "Not a hunch, Al. You've been spooked ever since we left for work. What's going on? If you tell me more government bullshit, I'll kill you. And what the hell was up with Luc-I-Am-The-Devil-In-Person?"

Shit. Only if she knew how right she was on that last point.

"Take a shower with me," I say, changing the subject. God, I want his tainted scent off her.

Her small hands rest at her hips and she glares at me. "Stop. Right now. I have been far too lenient with you, but I have to protect myself at some point, Al."

I sigh and yank my shirt off. Her eyes drop to my chest for a moment, but then they're back on mine, still questioning me.

"We'll talk in the shower, baby."

She huffs but stalks past me toward the bathroom. I follow after her, depositing the rest of my clothes and shoes along the way. My cock thickens when I see her pull her dress up over her head, and her tiny ass slightly jiggles in her black panties before she disappears into the bathroom. By the time I make it in there, she's started the shower and is completely naked. I glance in the mirror and see the fatigue and worry in my eyes. Diverting my eyes back over to her the moment the nausea churns my stomach, I stare at her beautiful body which soon settles my stomach.

With a kick, I shut the bathroom door and climb into the small shower with her. Her eyes are on mine, full of questions, as the water soaks her hair. I'm slightly distracted by the way the water is rolling down her beautiful breasts, but I know I have to give her something.

"Come here," I instruct. If I'm going to speak to her about things I feel uncomfortable speaking about, I want her close.

When she steps forward, I envelop her in a tight embrace. My palm strokes her back under the hot spray. God, why can't things be easy for us?

"I love you," I remind her.

An annoyed huff. "Crazy boy, you can't love me yet."

I do though. Whether or not she wants to believe it.

"I can too and I do. That's what got me into this mess in the first place."

She lifts her head to look up at me. "Mess?"

I hold her stare for several moments and drink in her every feature. If time would just hold still for one damn minute, I could freeze this moment and keep it in my memory bank forever. I may not have had any memories when I became a Minder, but I sure as shit will have memories now. They'll all be about her. I will die to protect those memories—no matter what happens between her and me.

"What if I told you I was sent here to look after you?" I question finally.

Her brows furrow. "I figured that one out on my own. Did the government really send you? Does this have to do with my husband?"

I wince when she says the word "husband" but shake my head no. "Actually, this is a private sector." I sigh. "Lark, you have to promise me something. Whatever I tell you has to stay here in this shower. Anything I reveal to you could destroy not only me, but us."

My words are cryptic, but she senses my seriousness because she nods.

"Tell me, Alpha."

With a rush of anxious breath, I tell her.

Lark

HE'S LOOKING DOWN at me as if it will physically pain him to say the words. It only further piques my curiosity. I don't press him, and he finally begins his story.

"Several years ago, I was recruited to do a very important job. They considered me heroic and one who possessed qualities perfect for the job of guarding people."

Okay . . .

"We're more or less in training mode until we're given our final assignment. Then, we can advance and become what we've worked so hard to achieve."

I frown. "It sort of sounds like government work."

He shakes his head. "It's not. However, I work for a very good company. Only the best work there. My job, though, requires me to protect people until our sister company takes over the guardianship but the people I protect aren't the good ones. Make sense so far?"

No.

"Not really. I sense that you are being purposely vague, but I'll take it for now," I say as I run my fingers down his spine.

His eyes briefly close, but when he reopens them, he continues his explanation. "Well anyway, it doesn't matter. I had a job to do. Lark, you were my job."

Were.

"But I'm not now?" I question with a pout.

Dipping down, he chastely kisses my lips. "Baby, I will die to protect you. But that's the problem. You were supposed to be a part of my job, but now, I want to tell them all to fuck off because you're all that matters to me."

"So quit," I tell him simply. "That weirdo Luc said he had a job for you. Can't you work for him?"

He groans. "I can't just quit. These people don't just let you quit. I'm not sure what they'll do, but I fear my life might be on the line for betraying my superiors to be with you. Besides, Luc is *not* one of the good guys."

Life on the line.

The bathroom spins and I sway in his arms.

"Shit! What's going on, Lark? Are you okay?" he demands as he presses me against him, so that my cheek rests on his chest.

I can't formulate words though. I cannot go through this shit again. A tear rolls down my cheek, and my nose burns with more unshed tears. My breaths are shallow as the dizzy waves won't stop.

"Lark!"

I finally drag my head up to look at him again. The worry on his face warms me and scares me all at once.

"They'll k-k-kill you?" I sputter out.

"God, I hope not, baby. That's the thing. I don't know what their plans are. There's another part to this though."

I can't handle any more sides to this.

"Let me wash you and I'll tell you in bed," he coos.

My knees wobble beneath me as I nod. I need to sit down for this. The teensy-weensy heart inside me threatens to nosedive off the steepest cliff.

He washes our bodies and my hair while I stare at him, numb. I hardly even process that he turns off the shower and bundles me up in a towel—I just know I'm suddenly dry.

"I'm taking you for a ride, Twiggy," he murmurs before scooping my body into his arms.

I rest the side of my face on his shoulder and inhale him. He may smell like soap, but he also smells like him. His scent is comforting and safe. I love his scent.

He strides out of the bathroom and into my room. Gently, he sets me down and removes my towel first before his. As I crawl into the bed and under the covers, I look at the man whose presence fills every square inch of my quaint bedroom. He's quite beautiful naked. If he weren't moving, I'd swear he were a perfect statue created only for me. With a sad smile, he climbs in after me, disturbing my unusual thoughts, and covers my naked body with his so he can look into my eyes. His elbows rest on either side of me so his entire weight isn't crushing me.

"What's the other part of this whole mess?" I finally ask. My voice sounds braver than I feel.

His normally kissable lips press together in a firm, anxious line. "The other company that is supposed to take over your guardianship is the bad company."

I stare at him and blink several times as I process his words. "Wait. Why does some bad company want to watch over me? I didn't do anything wrong!"

"I know, baby. That's the fucking problem. This is all a clusterfuck. Everything they told me about you is wrong. You don't deserve this. And now that I know this—*know how perfect you are*—I can't let them come near you. I swear to God I will die to protect you, Lark."

His words slice me open again.

"S-stop with the dying talk, Al. I can't fucking take it," I sob. More tears roll down my cheeks as I push away any thought of losing this man too. I can't take any more loss. I simply can't.

"I'm sorry," he whispers and presses a soft kiss on my lips. "I love you, Lark. Both companies can kiss my ass. I'll kill anyone who even looks at you wrong. Do you understand that? I. Will. Kill. Them."

I believe he will. His black eyes are pulsating with anger, and I'm glad I'm under his protection.

"Why do they want me?"

"I don't know, but they won't get you, baby."

I sniffle and process his words before coming up with more questions. "So, the timeline is three months? Now, we have two left? Maybe we can run away," I suggest hopefully.

He growls, and I sense that things may have changed. "Those were the original plans, but I've been alerted to the fact that I have a week to make a decision before all Hell breaks loose—literally."

My eyes dart back and forth, searching his for answers. A week? Holy shit. That's not enough time.

"What decision?"

His eyes fall shut as he brushes his lips against mine. "The bad company wants me to work for them. They've literally promised me the world, but they're known for being liars. I don't trust them one bit. We're on our own, baby."

"What about Omar and Lovenia? Do they know about this? Can they help us?"

He shakes his head. "Lovenia works for *them.* And *Omar* is my partner. His real name is Omega."

Omar is Omega. Lovenia works for them.

"I knew I hated that bitch," I snip out. "But wait? Oma—Omega worships the ground she walks on."

He nods sadly. "Like I said, Lar. It's just me and you, baby."

Surely there has to be someone who can help us. None of this makes sense.

"Can anyone help us?" I wonder aloud. My mind flits to my mom and dad, but I know they would be useless for this sort of thing. Mom works part time at their church as a secretary, and Dad is a professor at UCLA. Those two wouldn't know the first thing about competing agencies going after their daughter.

"There may be someone. Father Lester mentioned something to me that day we went to the church. I think he may be able guide us in the right direction," he says in a hope-filled voice. "Tomorrow, we can go see him. I'll swing by my old place and pick up your file. Maybe, together, we can find some answers."

I hug my hands around his back and wiggle my legs out from beneath him. The need to be close to him is strong. He just revealed some very important information, and I feel more connected to him somehow.

"After that, we go to my parents' house. They'll provide us a safe shelter."

His eyes widen in surprise. "You want me to meet your parents? What if they don't like me?"

A soft giggle escapes me. Only Alpha would be worried about my parents' impressions of him in the midst of the chaos we're dealing with.

"Don't worry. They'll love you. It's me I should be worried about. I haven't seen them in a very long time."

His black eyes soften and they almost seem grey. "You're just misunderstood, but you're very easy to love. I'm sure it will be fine, Twiggy," he teases. His cock twitches against me, which makes me grin.

"You're not so bad yourself, Al."

His face falls a bit and causes my heart to seize up. I want to give him those words—yet at the same time, those words belong to someone else. Alpha may have my body and that tiny piece of my heart, but he will never have those words. The problem is that, deep down, I know I'm lying to myself. Each time he tells me that he loves me, I physically have to swallow down the knee-jerk response to tell him the same, because I do love him. And that scares the shit out of me.

Loving him changes me.

Loving him means I was never Connor's true soul mate—that I let him down.

Loving him means taking my heart from my husband and giving it to Al.

I want to give Alpha those words one day, but not now. I've barely admitted it to myself, so I surely don't have the courage to utter them aloud. But there is something I can give him. Something I have desperately wanted to give to him for some time now.

"Roll over, big boy," I command saucily.

His melancholy face morphs into a silly one as he does as he was told. I sit up and admire the amazing man stretched out taking up most of my bed. The dark, wet hair on top of his head is beginning to dry, and it sticks out in a million different directions, making him look incredibly adorable yet fuckable at the same time.

"You're a feisty little thing. You know that, woman?" he laughs.

I beam at him but don't give him an answer. Instead, I slide down the bed until I'm positioned above one of his best assets. His eyes widen in realization, and a tremor quivers through him when I grasp his length. A little blow on the glistening tip causes him to groan out my name.

"I'm hungry, Al." I pretend pout. "I wish I had something to taste."

"Damn you, evil woman. You're a tease," he growls and slips a hand into my hair. His grip is firm, but he doesn't move me—he just holds on for dear life.

I dart my tongue out, my eyes never leaving his molten ones, and slowly taste him from the base of his cock up the shaft until I make it to the tip. With a flick, I lick the bead of pre-cum and find that he tastes both sweet and salty. Before I take him fully into my mouth, a wicked half grin tugs at my lips.

"Hold on there, Just Al. I'm about to take *you* for a ride."

As I slide my open mouth over his impressive cock, I am distracted for just a short while. Right now, the only thing that exists is the two of us.

My mouth and his cock.

His flesh and mine.

One tiny, throbbing, black heart. One big, strong pounding one big enough for two.

Just Al and Lark Miller.

Forever . . . *in this moment.*

Chapter Twenty-One

Alpha

I CAN'T BELIEVE I'm taking her to HEA Corp. But we need the file. I need to talk to Father Lester. We need to figure this shit out.

As we ride across town in the cab, I squeeze her hand. She's been thoughtful during the drive as she looks out the window, clutching on to the backpack in her lap. I wish I had access to her mind.

"We're almost there," I mutter aloud.

She nods without taking her eyes from the window. Honestly, I'm surprised she's still here. Last night, when I spilled what I could, I'd expected her to run for the hills. Instead, she took it like a champ, overlooking my dusting over the whole "angels and demons" aspect.

And then.

Holy mother of God.

And then she gave me a blow job sinful enough that would have likely made even Luc I. Furr himself drop to his knees and beg for mercy. Not only was she the first blow job I've ever had—*I think*—but she gave me the best. That part I just know.

The cabbie pulls in between the nondescript sister buildings and stops. I toss him a wad of bills and help Lark out of the car. Everything that has value to her is in the backpack she hands to me. This morning, before we left, she pulled her box down and wrapped up a framed ultrasound picture in a T-shirt that was also inside. When she lifted a photo album and I looked at her curiously, she quickly shoved it into the bottom of the bag along with a few other items. She ended up leaving an empty jewelry box but took the two wedding rings inside and slipped them on the chain of her cross. After tossing a few changes of clothes and her purse inside, she was ready to leave her apartment behind. She can't stay there anymore if I have any hope of saving her.

It sickens me that all she has in this life fits in that bag.

She has me now though, and I don't fit in the damn bag.

"I've passed by here a million times. Who knew?" she asks mostly to herself.

"Come on. Keep your head down and follow me. We'll get in and get out," I instruct as I take her hand once she's put on her backpack.

We slip into the building, and thankfully, nobody is hanging around in the lobby. As I escort her over to the elevators and hit the button to go up, I take another brief scan to make sure nobody is watching. If I can make it in and out without running into Pallas, I'll be doing great. With a ping, the doors open and we make it inside undetected. A rush of relieved breath escapes me as I glance down at Lark and wink at her. She looks cute as hell in her black tank that says, *Bad is the new good.*

"I love you, Twiggy," I blurt out. With this woman, weird shit comes out of my mouth all of the time. It's true though, and I'll tell her until I take my last breath.

She smiles back at me. "I know, big boy."

When the elevator opens to the second floor, I pull her behind me. Here, we'll have more trouble passing through unnoticed. This is the Minder's quarters when they're not out on assignment, and there's always someone walking around. I hurry us down the hallway until I find Omega's and my unit and punch in my code—1818—to get in.

I flick on the light near the door and see that everything appears just the same. Our single window overlooks the alley between the two HEA and HEL buildings. Both beds are in shambles because we're guys and guys don't make beds. No pictures or decorations adorn the walls or surfaces. At the end of each twin bed is a desk with a laptop and piles of papers. I release Lark's hand and stalk over to mine, which is closest to the window. Her file sits on top.

"Here it is," I tell her. "Turn around and we'll put it in your bag."

She raises a brow. "Al, I want to see."

My mind quickly checks through what I remember being in the file. I don't think anything can incriminate me and what I truly am, so I hesitantly hand it to her.

"Listen, Lar, this file is bullshit. I know that now. So please don't get upset with me."

She frowns but nods. Once she takes it from me, she sits down on my bed and flips it open. The "drug-addicted" picture of her is clipped to the front.

"I remember taking this picture," she whispers in a sad tone.

I sit beside her, wrap an arm around her, and pull her to me. "Were you on drugs?"

Her hollow laugh sends a chill down my spine. "Actually, yes. That was the day of Connor's memorial service. I could barely function, so my mother made me take something the doctor had prescribed and was safe for the baby to calm my ass down. Mom knew I would hate to miss the final goodbye to him and I wouldn't ever go if I continued throwing up and sobbing hysterically, so she pretty much forced it down my throat. God that was a sad day."

Drug-addicted. Those motherfuckers lied to me.

She flips the pictures up and begins reading every negative thing about her. Things I now know are made-up bullshit.

"These people you work for make me sound evil." She sighs with a ragged breath. "Alpha, I'm not evil. I might be a bitch. I might have a heart the size of my thumb. But I am not evil."

I kiss her head with reverence. "Baby, you are far from evil."

"Death-obsessed and satanic? What the fuck?" she explodes. "Drug-addicted. Negatively influences small children. This is sick, Al. Fucking sick. And unfuckingtrue!"

I hug her tight against me. "Yes, baby, I know. I'm so sorry."

"For the record, I have my reasons for being the way that I am. My dad is a professor at UCLA. He teaches religion and modern critical thought in the fall and topics in philosophy of religion in the spring. Since I was a baby, all I've ever heard about were his ramblings on theology. It was sort of ingrained in me," she reveals. "And my mother oversees funeral services at her church. I grew up running around caskets with dead people while Mom decorated the church or worked on the service pamphlets. I was a kid who grew up around death and continually learned about afterlife. Death-obsessed? Only one person on this planet could get away with teasing me on the matter, and ironically, he's dead. *But these people*—they can go fuck themselves."

Holy shit.

"They're wrong about you, Lark. That's what I'm trying to tell you. There must be some sort of error on their part, because none of this makes sense. Until it figures itself out, if that can even happen, I'll take you away from here and keep you safe." My voice is a solemn promise.

She slams the file shut and turns to me with tears in her eyes. "I'm so over this life."

Her words rip through my chest, and I want to vomit—and there's not a mirror in sight.

I take the file from her and set it beside me. "You can't mean that, Twiggy. *I'm* in this life."

Tears roll out and she presses her eyes shut. I raise my thumb to her cheek and wipe away a tear.

"Sometimes, Al, I wish I weren't here. All this life has ever provided was confusion, then heartache and more confusion, and in the end, I know there will be more heartache. I can feel it all the way down to my toes. Now, as all of this comes out, I understand why. You'll be taken from me just like he was. I'm not equipped to be in this life. God messed up when he made me. I'm a fucking defect of a human."

I growl out my disagreement, but she shakes her head no.

"I'm right. By the end of the week, you'll be dead and I'll be wherever the fuck life decides to plant me next. But rest assured, I'll be confused and heartbroken. Just like always," she sobs.

I help her slide her backpack down off her shoulders and place it on the floor. "Baby, you have to have hope. You can't assume the worst. I'm not going anywhere."

She chuckles darkly at me. "Big boy, I gave hope up a long time ago. Hope was stolen away from me the moment death took my husband and then my baby. Hope fucking sucks."

Leaning in, I kiss her lips and try to wordlessly convey that things will be okay. We need to get the fuck out of here before we're caught, but I need to somehow prove to her that I'm not going anywhere.

Breaking away from her lips, I tell her fiercely, "I love you, Lark Miller. We're in this together—until the very end."

A single tear rolls down her cheek as she nods at me. Whether or not she wants to believe it, I see it lying there just below the surface—the hope, the love. She may think I'm insane because my heart and soul decided to fuse themselves to hers, but she's just as guilty even though she's too afraid to voice it.

"What if the end is tomorrow?" she questions.

"Then, Twiggy, we're going to carpe fucking diem."

"We're almost there," I call out over my shoulder. After we sneaked back out of HEA, we took a cab to the diner and grabbed a quick lunch. Now, we are trotting to the church with my Lark on my back.

As we approach the church, a dirty, homeless man steps in front of us. "Can you spare any change? Do you have any food?"

The man is tall and incredibly bony. All I have is sixty bucks left in my wallet, and I had hoped to use that for cab fare to head to Lark's parents' house across town. But the sadness mixed with the glimmer of hope in his eyes has me easing Lark to her feet and fishing for my wallet.

I pull out all three twenties and hand them to him. "Sorry, buddy. This is all I have."

He grins broadly at me. I expect to see missing teeth, but instead, his smile is radiant. The man must still take care of his oral hygiene even while being homeless. If I had more time, I'd want to hear his story. He looks as if he needs someone to lend him an ear.

"Thank you, kind sir. You have no idea how this will help me," he says, his voice gracious. "And please call me Clarence."

I hear Lark unzip her bag, and she retrieves a package of Oreos. The smile on my lips is instant.

"Oreos are their own food group, Clarence," she tells him as she hands him the cookies and winks at me.

When he reaches for her, my protective guard goes up, so I watch him like a hawk. Without hesitation, she takes his hand with both of hers and shakes it.

"Good luck to you." She smiles before releasing him.

He beams at both of us once more. "God be with you both."

As we begin to walk away, I notice the man's dirty feet. "Where are your shoes?" I question.

"I don't have any."

He's about my size. I take my shoes off and hand them both to him. "Now you do."

The man's eyes brim with tears and he nods his thanks as he accepts them. We wave our goodbye to the man and walk hand in hand up to the church.

"Al, anyone ever told you you're an angel?" Lark asks.

My heart clenches with pain in my chest. It's a damn shame I'll never have the opportunity to be one. The sadness for this loss of my identity hurts so fucking much but the exchange more than makes up for it. Lark will always be worth it.

"I think you're the first," I tell her.

She squeezes my hand and flicks her green eyes, which are shining with pride, toward me. "Well, you are. You're like my very own guardian angel. Let's just hope you get to stick around."

She's right. I may not live past tomorrow. I for sure won't ever get my Seraph Guardian wings. But I'll protect and love her until my dying breath. With Lark, the rules don't matter.

The only thing that matters is her.

Chapter Twenty-Two

Lark

THE CHURCH IS empty, but all the lights are on. My shoeless guide leads me down the hallway toward Father Lester's office. Last time we were here, I wanted to crawl inside myself and hide—to disappear from the feelings Alpha had invoked in me. Now, I feel the slightest inkling of something so sinister that I want to go running back toward my internal safe haven. The niggling inside is a feeling I thought I'd eradicated from my life.

That feeling is hope. And I hate it.

"Let me do the talking," Alpha says with a crooked grin that makes my heart skip a couple of beats in my chest. The way his right brow rises in a playful way makes his black eyes seem dark blue, and with a smile that grows even broader, he almost reminds me of . . .

"Is everything okay?" Father Lester questions as he steps out of the doorway of his office. His eyes flit over to me, and I don't miss the disdain in them. It's clear he thinks I'm not good enough for Alpha. And while he may be right, it still hurts.

"Actually, no," Al sighs.

Father Lester groans but stalks back into his office. Yep—I've pissed off the preacher man just by being me. Story of my life.

I send Alpha an apologetic look, but he shakes his head and reaches for my hand. Because of Father Lester's obvious distaste for my relationship with Alpha, I'm hesitant to flaunt it in front of him, especially considering that he might be able to help us. When I don't accept his hand, he takes a step forward and steals my hand away anyway. Then he squares his shoulders and his features morph from anxious to resolved.

"Let's go, Twiggy."

As we enter together into the small office, I see Father Lester digging around in a cabinet with his back to us. Alpha leads me over to the two chairs in front of the desk and we sit down.

"These should fit," Father Lester grumbles as he tosses a pair of worn-out tennis shoes to Alpha, who catches them with ease and bends to put them on.

When my eyes meet the now angry ones of Father Lester, my heart sinks. What if he doesn't help us? What if this is just a waste of our very precious time?

Father Lester tears his eyes from mine as he walks around to the other side of the desk and sits in his chair. The air feels thick with tension as Alpha ties both shoes and sits up to face the man. His back is stiff and he seems prepared for battle.

"Father," Alpha begins, but he's silenced by the old man's raised hand.

"I know. You've clearly failed your final assignment. She's still alive though, which means you've done the unthinkable with her."

I bite my lip.

Alpha nods solemnly. "In a sense, yes."

Father Lester sends a glare my way but speaks to Al. "Son, I told you that if you were tempted by the woman, I could help you. Why didn't you come for my help sooner? You know I must turn you in now."

Tears well in my eyes. I knew coming here was a bad idea.

"Father, with all due respect," Alpha practically growls, "they were wrong. The file was wrong. There's some sort of mistake about Lark. She's not what they think."

Once again, Father Lester's eyes flicker over to me. He doesn't seem at all convinced. I'm sure that, in his eyes, I'm the epitome of evil, from my wild, dark hair, to my clothes, to every tattooed square inch of my flesh. Big, bad wolf here dressed like a black sheep.

"Son, it doesn't matter what the file says. You had a job to do. Your job had nothing to with investigating your assignment. The only job you had was to protect her until they came. And sleeping with her was certainly not part of the job."

I bite my tongue as a million rude remarks to this old man sit right on the tip of it, just waiting to be unleashed. Al seems to think we need him though, so I'll be quiet. For now.

"I know, but—" Alpha tries, but the old man waves him off again.

"But nothing, boy. You failed. Now I need to give Pallas a call. There are certain repercussions for your actions."

"Please, Father Lester," Alpha begs, "help me. They don't have to know. I've been remembering things . . ."

Father Lester's eyes darken at his admission. "Things? Like what?"

Alpha turns his gaze toward me and once again frowns in apology. "Like my name. Glimpses of my past. Small flashes of memories."

His name. A shudder courses through me at the reminder. He believes he shares the same name as my dead husband. The irony is not lost on me.

"I see."

"Before, when I was here," Alpha suddenly rushes out, "you said you began remembering your past. What did you do?"

Father Lester grumbles and leans back in his chair, but I don't miss the brief glimpse of sadness in his eyes. "I remembered my brother. Unfortunately, my brother was a bad man. Very evil. Our company was not wrong in their assessment of him."

"Wait. You were to protect your own brother and then handed them right over to the bad guys?" I demand harshly and interrupt their exchange.

Alpha curses under his breath and shoots me a look that says, *Shut up,* but I can't.

"Young lady, by you being here, listening to our business talk, so many rules have been broken. Poor Alpha will undergo the harshest of punishments all because of you and your evil temptress ways. You've stolen from this company someone who could have made a name for himself. Now—well—now, he'll be nothing but a disappointing waste of company resources."

A ragged breath rushes from Alpha, and I suddenly feel as if I'm the one protecting him. Standing quickly, I glower at the preacher man.

"You"—I point at him—"are the disappointment. You're supposed to be a man of God—someone who is supposed to have compassion and feels compelled to help those in need, yet there you are sitting in your chair like the pompous ass you are. Have you not even read the words in those books on the back of those pews in there? 'Bear one another's burdens, and so fulfill the law of Christ'—Galatians 6:2. Clearly, you're following the law of man and not the law here in this church. You sicken me."

The old man's eyes flash from anger to surprise. "You know the Bible?"

I roll my eyes at him. Because of my parents, I probably know more than he does. "I know a bit, and from what I know, you're nothing but a fraud. Come on, Alpha. Let's get out of here. He's not going to help us."

Alpha rises with reluctance, but his shoulders are hunched. He seems so dejected, and my little sliver of a heart breaks for him. This asshole in front of us singlehandedly broke down the man I love by making him feel like the scum of the Earth.

"I hope she was worth it, son. I hate that she was able to use her wicked ways to sway you from the path of good."

A woeful sound escapes Alpha, and I lose my mind. Before I can control myself, I scramble up onto the desk and slap the shit out of Father Lester.

"Lark!" Alpha growls as he slips a strong arm around my waist, hauling me back.

"You're an asshole!" I snarl at Father Lester. "This man is good—so good. How dare you think of him otherwise? He would do anything for anyone. Not just me, like you think. *Anyone.* His heart is so big that he shares it with everyone. You may think he's awful, but I thank God that I was able to help pull him away from your company's evil clutches. You're all twisted, and he was able to untangle himself from you. I *love* him and I'll protect him from the likes of you. Now, if you ever had any care for him at all, you'll give us a head start before you tattle to your superiors."

Father Lester, whose cheek is now smarting red, stares at me open-mouthed and in shock.

"You love me," Alpha whispers as he pulls my back to his chest and kisses the top of my head. "I knew it."

As much as my heart aches for the one I loved, it also throbs—filled with hope—as I finally verbalize what I knew all along. *That I love Just Al.*

He slides an arm over my shoulder and guides me away from the desk toward the door. We don't need the hypocritical preacher to help us. We have each other.

"If we hurry, I can call Dad and catch him on his way back from campus. He can pick us up on his way home," I tell him as we make it to the doorway. "Just tone it down on the 'Twiggy' stuff. It may have been several years since I last saw him, but my Dad will still be protective over me. Oh, and call him sir or Dr. Hutchinson—you'll be golden."

Dad is typically easygoing but I'm still nervous as hell about him meeting the only guy since Connor. And after all of these years, it might not be pretty.

"Dr. *Mathias* Hutchinson, a professor at UCLA?" Father Lester calls out in question.

Shit.

My head whirls back to look at him, but his hands are raised in surrender. I glare at him instead of answering. How in the fuck does he know my father? A worrisome thought enters my head. Between his job and my mother, Dad knows just about every church leader in a hundred-mile radius.

"I'll drive you to him," Father Lester mumbles grudgingly. "It appears there may be more here than meets the eye with you two."

A relieved sigh rushes from Alpha, and he hugs me. "We're going to fix this, Twiggy," he tells me with confidence.

My lips curl into the smallest of smiles. "I hope you're right, Al. I've given you my tiny heart. And though it may be little, it will need the most protection of all."

It feels good to hope again.

The entire ride over to Dad's office is a quiet one. Even though Father Lester suddenly decided to help us, I don't trust his intentions. His mood has become introspective while he's been driving, and we're in the back seat of his secondhand Ford Crown Victoria—an old police car complete with the black-and-white paint job. Al remains pensive as well as he holds my hand.

After we pull into the emptying staff parking lot and turn into a spot, I finally ask the question that has been plaguing me. "How do you know my dad, Father Lester?"

He chuckles as he puts the car into park and shuts it off. When he turns to look at me, he smiles, which is a little unnerving considering this is the first time he's aimed it my way.

"Your dad and I go way back. We used to work together."

"You worked at UCLA?" I question.

He shakes his head and climbs out of the car. Alpha and I exchange a glance before we get out and follow after him.

"Dad has only ever worked here," I call out after the bizarre old man and wave toward the building where my dad's office resides. "I guess I don't understand what you mean."

"There's a lot you don't understand. You are incapable of understanding. Just know that your father and I knew each other from *before*." The way he says the last part indicates something other than a time period and more along the lines of an event.

Alpha seems uncomfortable with our exchange as we trek after Father Lester. His demeanor has felt different since we stepped foot in that church earlier.

"Before what?"

Instead of giving me an answer, Father Lester wrenches the door to the building open and disappears inside.

"He's crazy, Al," I groan and shake my head. "None of it makes any sense, and he's not very forthcoming on his answers."

Alpha trots ahead of me and opens the door. "It makes sense to me, Twiggy. But, babe, I'm not sure if this is good news or bad news."

I stop in the doorway and give him a questioning look. "What do you mean?"

"If your dad used to work with Father Lester," he sighs, "then that means he's retired from the company I work for—the company we're trying to escape from. It means that your dad might not be any help at all. In fact, he may just help Father Lester drag our asses back to my boss, Pallas."

"No, he's my dad. It doesn't matter that we haven't spoken in years. He loves me and would never sell me out for some 'company' he supposedly worked for. Trust me," I explain vehemently.

Alpha slides a tender palm up my neck and strokes his thumb along my cheek. His coal-colored eyes are once again apologetic. I hate that he feels as if he has to take the brunt of everything we're going through. It's not his fault. Al is a good man.

"Twiggy, this company is bigger than we are. Bigger than anything I've ever known. Once you're married to this company, you don't simply get out. They always own a part of you, even in retirement."

I scowl at him. "He's. My. Dad. He'll listen to us—he'll help us, Al. You have to try and have a little faith."

Alpha throws a crooked grin my way and brings his lips close to mine. "I'll try and do anything for you, baby. I love you, Lark Miller."

With a soft kiss, he presses his warm lips against my own. I wrap my arms around his solid back and kiss him harder. Now that I've pledged my heart to him, I don't want to ever let him go. In a perfect world, this could be my eternity—me pressed firmly against the protective and statuesque man in my arms. We could stay here forever, bound by a simple kiss packed with so much love. Time could freeze us and I would be in complete bliss with that.

Happiness is such a foreign concept for me—a concept I didn't think I'd ever feel again. But with Alpha, broken pieces are being mended. Black hearts are showing signs of life. Love is a tiny seed deep in my soul that is beginning to break free from the compacted soil of my being and budding with growth.

With Al, I can be whole again.

I won't let anyone get in my way this time. Last time, the government stole my love away. Connor was married to their institution every bit as much as he was married to me. And even though Al may *think* he's married to his company equally powerful as our US government, I have other ideas.

I'm the tempting lover he had an affair with. I'm the one who stole him away. This time, I'm the one in control of my love—of my destiny.

It's time to plan a divorce.

"I love you too, Just Al. It's time to make you mine forever."

Chapter Twenty-Three

Alpha

I'LL NEVER GET tired of hearing those words. "*I love you too, Just Al.*" If only I could give her more of me—climb into the blankness that is my mind and find out who I truly am. Then she could love more than Just Al. She could love all of me, even the parts of me I don't even know.

"When you get big like me, you can fit the whole Oreo in your mouth like this," Daddy says with a smile before he pushes the whole cookie into his mouth.

His sandy-blond hair is combed over to the side, just like he always wears it to the office. Mommy says that he's the best salesman at his insurance company. He works long hours but takes good care of Mom and me. Sometimes, he brings me home a toy if I've been really good.

"I'm seven, Daddy. I'm big," I argue. Then I attempt to shove the entire dripping-with-milk-and-now-soggy Oreo into my mouth.

I make a huge mess, and Daddy laughs as he ruffles my hair.

"Are you feeding him dessert before dinner?!" Mommy gasps when she enters the kitchen. "Arnold, I oughta skin you alive for that!"

Daddy winks at me before smiling one of those big smiles that always makes her cheeks turn red.

"Baby doll, Oreos aren't dessert. They're their own food group—a daily necessity, if you will. He'll survive and eat his dinner too." When he turns back to me, he grins, "Right, big boy?"

"Right, Daddy!"

"Right, big boy?" Lark questions, causing my memory to fade into nothingness. We've finished our kiss, and she's staring at me with concern written all over her face.

"What? Sorry. I had a memory," I murmur as I close my eyes.

My mom was so beautiful with her long, light-brown hair and matching eyes. And my dad . . . He was handsome and charming. With my black hair and dark eyes, I look nothing like them.

"Of what?" Lark asks in a nervous tone.

I know she thinks I'm going to ramble more mumbo jumbo about my name being Connor because she pushes her shoulders back and lifts her chin a bit as if to physically prepare herself for my words. God, she's so brave.

"Of my parents. I miss them," I sigh. "Apparently, Dad loved Oreos just like you do." My lips curl into a small smile at the memory.

If I knew more about them, I could look for them. They would love Lark, I'm sure of it. But what if they're dead? The thought sickens me.

Her eyes widen in surprise. "Your dad loved Oreos?"

I chuckle. "He thought they were their own food group too. I think you two would really hit it off. Too bad I have no idea how to find them."

One tear escapes from her eye and rolls down her cheek before she takes a ragged gasp of breath. "Come on. Let's go see my dad."

She breaks away from me and strides with an unusual quickness for someone with such short legs down the hallway. When I catch up with her, I steal her hand with mine, threading our fingers together as we walk. As we approach the last door on the right, we hear hushed voices.

"In here." She points and leads me through the doorway.

Upon our entry, Father Lester and who I'm assuming is Dr. Hutchinson halt their whispers.

"Dad," Lark greets the man, confirming my conclusion. Her voice quivers a bit, but she is tough and swallows it down.

"Lark. I've missed you so much," he smiles with sudden tears in his eyes and then he raises both arms.

She hesitates, only for a moment, before bounding over to him. The bear hug he gives her nearly crushes her.

After they finally break apart, she introduces me to her father. "Dad, this is my—this is Al. Al, this my dad, Mathias."

Remembering my manners, I shake his hand with a firm grip. "Dr. Hutchinson," I nod.

He resembles Lark in the way that his hair is a wild, dark wavy mess on his head, but his eyes are the color of midnight, much like my own. After we finish the introductions, he regards me with curiosity.

"Call me Mathias. So Father Lester tells me you're in a little bit of trouble?" he asks.

"Yes, sir," I tell him with a rush of breath. "My final assignment was your daughter."

His eyes darken and his features become fierce. "Final assignment? You're a Minder? Not an SG?"

I nod solemnly. If he once worked for HEA like Father Lester indicated, he knows that the Minders only protect those destined for Hell. Hearing that your daughter is headed there can't be good news for any father.

Lark's eyes flicker with interest at learning a bit more about the "company," but she wisely stays quiet.

"Unfortunately, I'm a Minder. Well, was. Now, I'm not sure what will happen," I tell him.

His dark brows furrow together in confusion. "Why?"

Father Lester interjects. "You don't have to worry, Mathias. He broke the rules. Apparently, these two are in love now and he's not letting *them* take her. But, as you and I both know, that isn't going to sit pretty with his superiors."

I know that, by them, he means Hell. And he's right. I'll set fire to every inch of this Earth before I let anyone touch my girl.

"Well, damn. We have a problem here," Mathias murmurs. "Rules are rules."

My heart sinks. He sounds resolved, and it doesn't seem like he's in favor of helping us.

I straighten my back and meet his eyes. "With all due respect, sir, I understand the rules. I know that they are very good at what they do—

how they select their assignments. However, this time, they're wrong."

His eyes dart over to Lark, and then he looks back at me. I can see, just below the surface, the disbelief. He sees the troubled woman with the mouth of a sailor, countless tattoos, and the emotional baggage that creates the saddest fucking aura around her. And even though she's his daughter, he doesn't seem convinced that I'm right. He assumes his daughter is destined for Hell. Well, fuck him too.

"They. Are. Wrong," I growl. "She's not evil. Everything in her file is a fucking lie. I don't understand why they would put made-up bullshit in there, but none of it is true. She's a good person, and I'll kill anyone who tries to take her away from me."

Mathias's eyes narrow as he searches mine for any deception, but my words are honest. I'm one hundred percent convinced they are all wrong.

Finally, he nods his understanding. "This doesn't happen a lot, but it does happen. We'll need to lie low until we get this sorted," he instructs as he stalks over to his desk to grab his briefcase.

"Dad, why didn't you ever tell me you worked for some bad company?" Lark asks. "Is it the government? I thought it had to do with Connor, but now, I'm not certain. Are they targeting me because of you? None of this makes any sense!"

It doesn't make any sense because she doesn't have all the facts. And I can't just come right out and tell her that I'm an angel-in-training who's dead set on keeping her out of Hell. She'll lose her damn mind.

"Lark, we don't have time for all of this. This company is a good company, but they, much like any company, have errors from time to time. That's why we need stay under their radar while we gather the necessary facts and take the proper steps to fix this. I never told you because this company requires the utmost secrecy. Your mother doesn't even know about it, and I'd like to keep it that way. Are we clear?" Mathias's authoritative voice booms.

Lark frowns but nods. "Fine, but I can't lose Al too. Losing Connor and then the baby nearly killed me. I love him just like I loved my husband—I'll never recover if they take him from me."

"I love him just like I loved my husband."

My eyes fall to the wedding bands on the chain of her cross necklace around her neck. Right now, in the small office, in the midst of our chaotic situation, I know that I want to be her husband one day. I want her to wear my ring on her finger. To carry my last name . . . if I had one.

She's my destiny.

She's my forever.

After an emotional reunion between Lark and her mother, Bea, we sit down to a spaghetti dinner and enjoy each other's company. It is surreal to feel as if I am a part of a family, even if only for a moment. I'm not sure if I'll ever find my parents again or that I'll even be guaranteed a tomorrow, but in this moment, I have a family.

We all have to pretend for Bea's benefit—who thinks Lark just had a change of heart and wanted to reconnect with family after all of these years. She thinks I work at the church with Father Lester, which isn't far from the truth. After dinner is over and Bea takes Lark back to the bedroom to talk in private, the three of us men launch into a discussion.

"What do we do, Mathias? How can I get HEA to understand they've made a mistake?" I question.

He frowns. "I've been thinking about this. Al, there's something you need to know."

I glance over at Father Lester, who doesn't seem at all surprised at what Mathias is about to tell me. "Okay, so spill."

"Pallas was my partner," he begins.

My stomach flops. "No shit? Wow. Okay and?"

"And things, like for you, went to Hell in a hand basket during my final assignment too."

I know I shouldn't feel hopeful, but the butterflies have already begun to flutter around in my belly. Things went wrong for him, but he's still alive and kicking. Furthermore, he has a career and family, too. Doesn't seem too bad.

"Anyway," he continues, "they made a mistake on the person I was to protect as well. They'd said she was going to commit murder. That she was an evil young woman who was slowly poisoning her father."

I want to shake him and tell him to hurry up with it, but instead, I grit my teeth together and wait.

"Well, I met this vile woman. She was beautiful and tempting as could be. Every time she smiled, I had the urge to kiss her despite her evil ways."

A small grin tugs at my lips because that's exactly how I felt with Lark.

"But as much as I wanted to kiss her, I knew she was nothing more than a bad person who needed to be kept alive until the Reapers came for her. Every day, time just ticked away and I couldn't wait to get my wings. I thought I had the assignment in the bag until *it* happened."

"It?"

His voice is furious with his next words. "I used to hide in the shadows around her house and peek in the windows to make sure she was still alive. When I heard screams, I ran to the window and was sickened by what I saw." He closes his eyes and shakes his head as if to rid himself of the visual. "Her father was sloppy drunk but was whipping his belt around in the air at her mother. From my position, I could see the black eye of her mother. The bruises. And just as I thought he was going to pound the tar out of his wife with that belt, my assignment stepped in. She screamed at him to get his attention off her mother and onto her. That day, I watched in horror as that man beat my assignment."

Now I'm angry. "Why didn't you stop him? You just stood there and watched him beat her up?"

He holds up a palm to quiet me. "I couldn't blow my cover, but suddenly, things became clearer. I began to really watch my subject. When they had said she was practicing witchcraft, I discovered that she was really at the library learning about ways to poison the man who abused her and her mother, not learning stupid spells. Where the file said she was stealing money from her parents to feed a drug habit, I learned through investigation that her mom was giving her money to stash away for them so they could run away from that monster. When the file mentioned that she was a jobless college dropout, I understood that she had to do what she could to protect her mother. The file told a story of loss of virginity at age fifteen, but what it didn't tell was that he was the one who'd taken it. It was all a fucking mistake, Al."

His eyes are brimming with outraged tears, and his fists clench until the knuckles turn white. "My subject was nothing but an innocent. A damn innocent, and they were going to have those asshole Reapers take her to Hell, where she didn't belong. I was livid once I discovered the truth. It took everything in me not to murder the motherfucker myself. When I confided in my partner, Pallas, he thought I'd lost my mind. But I showed him my proof. Together, we went through the proper channels and were awarded a meeting with upper management. They weren't too keen on the idea that they'd made a mistake, at first. It took days for them to pick through all of my evidence. Finally, though, they had to admit they were wrong."

So maybe there is hope for Lark and me.

"And then what happened? Did you become a Seraph Guardian?" I ask.

He shakes his head wistfully, but I don't see any regret in his eyes. "No, son, I did not. Apparently, even though I'd done the right thing in bringing the error to their attention, I was in the wrong for investigating in the first place. To become a true Seraph Guardian, you need to be focused, task driven, emotionless. I let my emotions get involved and I wanted to truly save her, not just as a part of my job. But forever."

"Bea was your final assignment?" I question.

His smile is immediate. "Yes, and it was the best thing I ever did. But because I'd fallen for her, I would never be able to move on and truly be what I'd worked so hard to become. I wasn't a failure, so I didn't belong over at HEL, but I also didn't belong at HEA. They let me out of the program on a technicality—the technicality being that they didn't know what the hell to do with me. I hadn't broken any laws or anything, so they just allowed me to leave. It was unprecedented. At first, I was confused and frustrated, not really knowing what to do or where to go. I ended up teaching at UCLA what HEA said was okay for me to teach and made a career of it. Bea and I married not long after and then she was pregnant with Lark. It worked for us."

It will work for us too. I feel like fist-pumping the fucking air right now.

"This is good news, Mathias. Let's set up a meeting with upper management so we can tell them about Lark—explain that they've done it again, just like with Bea." I'm grinning like a fool.

"Al, I hadn't broken any rules, remember? They didn't know what to do with me. But I'm afraid you have, haven't you?"

Thou shalt not fornicate with final assignment. If Minder fornicates with final assignment, they will be terminated from the program and banished from HEA Corp property. HEL will become administrator over failed Minder, whom shalt now be called Reaper.

I scrub my cheeks with my palms in frustration. All Minders know the rules of their final assignment. Being one of the best, I have the rules fucking memorized. I didn't just sleep with her once. I slept with her over and over again. Hell, I'd do it again right now if we were alone.

"Fuck!" I bark. "What do we do, then? They're still wrong. I won't let a Reaper take her to Hell, because she doesn't belong there. She belongs with me. Is there a place I can take her to hide?"

Mathias frowns and exchanges a glance with Father Lester, who's been quietly listening to his story. "Al, there's nowhere to hide. They're probably following you as we speak—watching your every move. While we'll most likely be able to change Lark's future, yours is fairly certain. The moment they get ahold of you, son, you'll meet your fate. You've broken a very clear rule of theirs, and they carry out their punishments strictly."

Just weeks ago, I had my eyes on a pair of wings and joining the ranks of HEA's most elite. Now, I'm destined to work for Luc and Corson, just like those two seemed to have predicted.

"I won't do it. I won't work for those bastards. I fell in love—I didn't commit murder. There's no way I'll ever willingly step foot over there," I tell him in a firm tone.

Mathias looks away as if he doesn't want to utter his next words.

So Father Lester speaks up instead. "You won't have a choice. They will come for you, and there will be no stopping it when it happens. I'm sorry, Alpha. You're a good kid, but they have rules and you broke them. You may as well accept your fate. The two of you will never be together."

I fold my arms across my chest and look him square in the eye. My jaw clenches as the fury of my situation ebbs and flows just under my skin, along my bones.

"I will not accept that fate. Ever. They'll have to kill me first."

Mathias finally turns his attention back to me. "Son, they can and they will. You should leave Lark before it gets too messy. My daughter has been through enough. I'm not sure she can take losing another love—she barely survived it the first time. If you leave and go to them, at least she'll know you're alive. But if they kill you"—he sighs with sadness—"I am certain that will kill her."

Chapter Twenty-Four

Lark

"WHAT DID THEY say? Can they help you?" I finally ask as we curl up together under the covers in my old room. I know the men talked tonight while Mom attempted to catch up with me on how I was doing. Even though I was glad to see her after all these years, I was distracted by wondering what they were discussing.

He's propped up on one elbow and looking down at me with a frown. "They can't help me. I broke a rule, Twiggy. Since I 'fornicated' with you, they won't help me. Your dad and Father Lester are sure they'll drop your case, but I'm screwed."

Fornicated?

"You're fucking kidding me right now. Because we aren't married and slept together, they can't help you?" I snarl. "That's the dumbest damn thing I've ever heard. What kind of archaic company do you work for? This is stupid. Let's go to the police, the FBI—anyone!"

His eyes close and he leans forward, brushing his lips against mine. "Lar, it's not that easy. You don't understand."

Of course I don't understand. It's fucking ridiculous. "Make me understand. Stop being so damn vague and come out with it. I can handle it, Al. Just tell me. How are we supposed to fix this if you can't even be straight with me?"

Blinking his eyes open, he pins me with a serious and certain stare. "I. Want. To. Tell. You."

I look at him in disbelief, as if he's lost a few brain cells. "Then tell me, big boy."

He groans but exhales in resignation. "Promise me, then. Promise me that, when I come out with this wildly outrageous story, not only will you believe me, but you'll also still love me."

"Of course. Tell me." I give him the words, but unease begins to tendril through my veins. Just like when he revealed his snippets of memories, I feel as if I'm not going to like his words. When he told me about how his father loved Oreos, I nearly died. It brought up sad memories of Connor—memories I can no longer deal with.

"Twiggy, I work for HEA Corp."

I stare at him with a look that urges him to proceed.

"Luc owns HEL Enterprises."

And? Again with the impatient look.

"I'm a Minder in training to be a Seraph Guardian."

"I remember Dad speaking about that. Are you all spies? I would assume you work for the CIA or something, but maybe you are a part of an espionage ring instead. What country did you come from?" I demand.

He frowns and shakes his head. "This is more outside the scope of reality. Twiggy, you weren't far off when you said I was your guardian angel. I was actually training to be one."

Guardian angel? A giggle bubbles in my chest and bursts out.

Threading my fingers through his hair, I pull him to me for a kiss. "Just Al, you're cute. But seriously, tell me the truth."

His face is serious. No smiles. No humor. No playfulness. "I was supposed to watch you until your death, which was set for three months out of my start date. You were my final assignment, and upon completion, I was to get my wings."

"I want wings. That's all I ever wanted."

Everyone wants fucking wings.

Shit.

"After the three months were over and if I had kept you alive, I would get those wings. HEL would send a Reaper for you and take you to Hell. You were supposed to be bad. But, Twiggy, you aren't. You are beautiful. Kind. Bighearted. You have an innocence below your jagged façade. You're more than what meets the eye. Your file is a fucking mistake. You're my angel, Lark, and I won't let them hurt you."

No.

No.

No.

"Al, this isn't funny," I whisper.

"No, it's not," he agrees with a sigh.

Shit. "This, um, seems a little out there, but say I buy your story. What does that mean for you? Since you fornicated with me and all . . ." I trail off.

"It means I'll be sent to work for Luc at HEL. I'd rather die than work for them," he growls.

He'd rather die.

"Don't say that," I choke out.

"You don't understand. I will not work for the Devil. They can kill me, but I won't go willingly. Everything about him and his company goes against everything ingrained in me. Like you, I'm not a bad person, either. Lark, I don't deserve to be punished. I deserve you."

A tear rolls out, which he swipes away with his thumb.

"But you can't have me?" I sob.

He shakes his head with despondency. "They won't let me have you."

This is a sick, cruel world we live in.

Suddenly, a thought bursts into my head. "Wait! Luc said I could work for him and then we could be together, Al. Don't you see? That could be our out."

A deep growl rumbles through his chest. "No. Absolutely fucking not. They're liars, Twiggy. They will tell you what they know you'll want to hear to get you to sign the dotted fucking line. I won't let a good soul like you join the ranks of them. People like us don't belong there."

My thoughts are scattering around in every which direction in my head like a herd of cats. There has to be an answer. We have to find a way to get him off the hook. When Alpha begins kissing my neck, my mind becomes vividly clear. The only thing that resides inside is him.

“Make love to me, sweet Lark, for this could be our last night together,” he murmurs, his hot breath fanning against my flesh.

A chill, partly full of terror from his words and partly laced with desire, slithers down my spine. As his tongue flicks the lobe of my ear, a whimper rushes out of me. He momentarily breaks away from me to push his boxers down his legs. Needing him infinitely, I part my naked thighs under my long shirt and hook his waist with my legs. Wordlessly, he enters me without warning.

“Al,” I moan against his mouth.

His response is a grunt of his own as he begins thrusting into me. The very idea of never being with him like this again seizes my heart. I can’t live without him. I just can’t. He pulled me from the dark, bitter hole I’d lived in and forced his sweet, protective love on me. I wasn’t immune to his charms and immediately succumbed to them. This man found me and fixed me the moment our eyes met.

“Lark, you’re mine forever, no matter what. Promise me,” he pants as he brings us closer to ecstasy with each movement within me. “’Til death.”

“’Til death.”

Another mournful sob catches in my throat, but he kisses it away.

“Al, I can’t promise that.”

A dejected sound echoes against the walls of my old bedroom. “Please, Twiggy. Forever,” he begs, our orgasms just on the horizon.

“I’ll promise you forever. Even *after* death—not just ’til.”

I ignore the fact that I’ve made this promise before. All that matters now is Alpha—the man I know I’ll never break that promise to.

“I love you, Lark Miller. Even after I take my last breath.”

“I love you too, Just Al. Even after I take my last breath.”

Our words might be just that—words. But as we both cry out when our climaxes shudder through us, I know we’ve made an unbreakable vow to each other. My soul threads itself intricately with his until it becomes one.

We’re Lark and Al.

Forever.

The sheets are cold.

My skin is cold.

The heart in my chest feels fucking frozen.

"Alpha?" I croak out into the dark. My throat is dry from sleep, so my voice doesn't carry far.

Silence.

Scrambling across the bed, I find the lamp and switch it on. The first thing I notice, aside from the apparent disappearance of Al, is the poem.

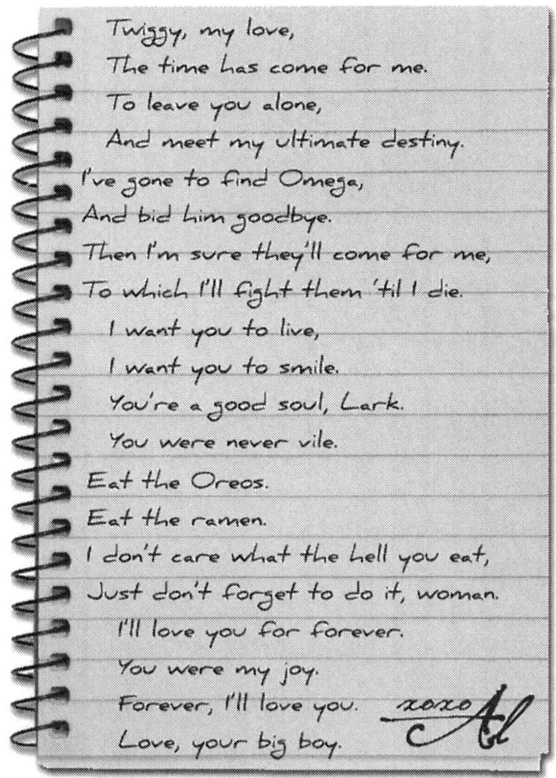

Twiggy, my love,
The time has come for me.
To leave you alone,
And meet my ultimate destiny.
I've gone to find Omega,
And bid him goodbye.
Then I'm sure they'll come for me,
To which I'll fight them 'til I die.
I want you to live,
I want you to smile.
You're a good soul, Lark.
You were never vile.
Eat the Oreos.
Eat the ramen.
I don't care what the hell you eat,
Just don't forget to do it, woman.
I'll love you for forever.
You were my joy.
Forever, I'll love you.
Love, your big boy.
xoxo
Al

No!

Bursting from the bed, I throw clothes on as quickly as possible. If

I can catch him, we can run away together. I won't let him go to HEL. And I certainly won't let them kill him.

I'm about to wake my parents and tell them that I'm borrowing their car when I hear a honk out front. Yanking up my purse, I slip out of my bedroom toward the front door. Then I peek through the window and see a cab sitting in the driveway.

What the hell?

Not one to miss an opportunity, I fling the door open and bound down the front steps toward the cab. The front window is rolled down, and the cabbie sticks his head out.

"Thought you might need a ride," a familiar voice calls out.

As I approach, the moonlight reveals the face of Clarence, the homeless man.

"You got a job?" I ask in surprise. His appearance is clean, and he seems proud as punch to be offering me a ride.

"Something like that. Climb in. I'll take you where you need to go."

I run over to the passenger's side and get in the front seat. "Where is it you think I need to go?" Even though I like Clarence, his arrival is too convenient.

"To your apartment to stop Alpha, of course."

"Who are you?" I demand as he begins backing out of the driveway. When he turns his gaze to me, I realize he's quite handsome all cleaned up.

"I'm Clarence, your guardian angel."

Guardian angel?

"I thought I was destined for Hell," I smirk as I cross my arms in defiance.

His laughter is infectious and light, like bells ringing, but I stubbornly refuse to join in.

"Dearest Lark, you *were* destined for Hell—that much is true. However, the instructions pertaining to you have changed. It would seem that your file was tampered with. And that, my friend, is an illegal, punishable offense on our end. But to be able to tamper with a human's file means someone of high authority was behind this. That is something that has everyone's attention. I've been tasked with keeping you safe."

My file has been tampered with. Why?

"Clarence?"

He cruises down the streets but doesn't look over at me as to not take his attention away from the road. "Yes, Lark?"

"Why would they choose my file to tamper with? What did I ever do to anybody?"

His eyes briefly flicker over to mine before he finds the road ahead of him again. "Dear, just like God's divine plan, others have their own plans. You could just be a tiny pawn—one small piece of a jigsaw puzzle—that brings them closer to their agenda. For all we know, this could have been premeditated for decades. Eras, even. Just know that, now that a pattern has been discovered, mysteries will begin to unravel. Haven't you ever heard the ol' familiar saying?" he chuckles. "The good guys always win. And you, Lark, just like Alpha, are the good guys. Have faith, sweet girl."

Have faith.

I do have faith. I've fought too long in this life—gone through way too much—to let it all be taken away from me because of some crook.

"Alpha said he'd broken one of the main rules." I look out the window as my cheeks redden. "We fornicated." Shit. Even the word sounds lame.

More bell-like laughing comes from the handsome angel. "Is that so, Lark Miller?"

Jerking my head over to him, I glare. "It is. Alpha said that—"

"Maybe Alpha doesn't know everything like I do . . ."

I chew on my lip, turn my attention back out the window, and watch the passing cars go by. My belly grumbles, and I fight off a wave of nausea. I guess the spaghetti is long gone from my system. Should have grabbed a . . .

"Care for an Oreo?" Clarence asks as he reaches behind my seat and pulls out the same package I gave to him yesterday.

"What is it about you people that you're so dead set on me eating?" I mumble but graciously take the package from him.

He laughs again, but this time, I join him with a small giggle.

"Clarence, I like you."

Grinning as he turns down the street that will eventually end up at my apartment in several miles, he says, "I like you too, Lark Miller."

As I eat my Oreos in comfortable silence with my guardian angel, a thought pops into my head. And now, after everything, I feel guilty for thinking it.

"I have a question for you, Clarence. If you're an angel, do you know . . ." I sigh and fight the urge to cry. "Do you know Connor? My baby? Are they okay? Happy?" A sob hangs in my throat, but I refuse to let it come out.

He reaches over and takes my hand, giving it a squeeze. "I do know them."

I look up at him as if to nonverbally tell him to please continue before I throttle him.

"Lark, they're fine. Okay? One day, you'll be reunited with your family. That's a promise."

Tears roll down my cheeks, and this time, I cry out into the silent car. But with this beautiful piece of information, confusion sets in and another loss grips my throat.

"What about Alpha? If I'm reunited with them, what will happen to him? I promised him forever."

Clarence squeezes my hand once more, and an ache in my heart eases. Something about his presence comforts me. "Sweet girl, if I told you everything, life would lose all mystery. How about this—Alpha will be happy. Is that enough? Can you live with that answer?"

The distance to the apartment becomes shorter and shorter as we get closer. I feel as if it's a metaphor for Alpha's and my relationship—the time is ticking away.

"So, if I can only have him until I see my family again, what's the point? Why are we going after him? It will only hurt him."

Clarence laughs with kindness at me. "Lark, *you* are Alpha's happiness. Both of you are threads in a carefully woven masterpiece of a blanket that is life. Parts of you are weaved into parts of him. There's no changing that."

His riddles confuse me, and I feel slightly dizzy. The Oreos are doing nothing to help me feel better. I'll be at ease once I'm wrapped up in Alpha's arms. My sweet Al. The man I'll only have for a blip of time before he's gone again. And then I'll see my family again.

But what about Just Al?

A strong ache in my chest threatens to rip me in half. Why is life so unfair? Why send me Al if only to tear him away from me once again? It just doesn't make sense. For now, though, I'll take what I can get of him. Whether it be one more day or ten more years. Clarence said that I was his happiness for the time being. I won't let Alpha run into the lion's den and let them kill him. I'll keep him as long as I can.

Twiggy and Just Al.

'Til death.

Chapter Twenty-Five

Alpha

LEAVING HER IN the middle of the night was the hardest thing I've ever had to do. But it had to be done. Mathias and Father Lester had made it clear. Lark is safe now. Her destiny will change because of the mistake. That meant she would be assigned a guardian angel.

It also means that I am no longer a part of her picture. My fate was to meet the consequences of my actions head on. In the morning, Father Lester and Mathias are taking my case to upper management to clear Lark's name. There would be nothing they would be able to do for me though. HEA will banish me to HEL. I will refuse to work for them. Luc or Corson will have to kill me. My soul will be forced to Hell.

But I'll never go willingly.

And I'll spend eternity with Lark's face, her voice, her sweet smell seared into my memory. They can try to wipe it from my brain, but as long as I exist, on whatever plane and in whatever capacity, I'll always have her memorized. I'll live happily ever after in my own right.

Lark is mine forever.

First, though, I must apologize to my best friend, Omega. I wasn't there for him. He could have helped me, but I'd chose to forge along on my own. And now . . . Now, he'll go on to be a Seraph Guardian alone. I let him down just like I let the love of my life down.

As I climb the steps to the second floor of Lark's apartment building, anxiety threatens to squeeze the air from my chest. I already miss her and it's only been long enough for me to hitch a ride over here. How will eternity without her feel?

It will feel fucking awful. That's how.

As soon as I reach the landing, my eyes meet the greasy ones of the same Reaper who has been hanging around these parts lately. It's another fucking reminder of how much I hate HEL and everyone there.

"Get the fuck out of here," I growl.

He laughs like a hyena but wisely skitters past me like the rat he is and descends the stairs. I make a beeline over to my apartment and push the door open. Omega is snoring in his room, so I stalk over there and switch the light on. Thankfully, Lovenia isn't here with him.

"Omega, get up," I bark.

He sits up and glares at me in confusion. "What the hell, Alpha? Why did you wake me up?"

Running my fingers through my hair, I groan. "Buddy, it's over. I've come to say goodbye."

Anger sets in as his naked ass springs from the bed and starts throwing clothes on. "What's over? And where the fuck is Love?"

My eyes skim the other side of bed, which was clearly abandoned by her. "I don't know where she is. But I'm over—that's what. I spoke to Father Lester and another old Minder named Mathias. Lark's file is a mistake just like I knew, and while she will be safe from HEL, I still broke one of the biggest Minder rules by sleeping with her. They both agree that I'm screwed."

He scowls and crosses his arms over his chest. "I've been talking to Love about this—about your situation with Lark. She told me Luc had offered you both jobs at HEL. If you take it, this will all be over. Love seems perfectly content working there. You could have your happy ending that way, Al."

I shake my head at him. "No. I won't work for them. Luc and Corson—they're all liars. The end has come for me, Omega, and it isn't happy."

He growls in frustration but is once again distracted by the absence of Lovenia. "Where in the fuck is my woman?"

"Dude, snap out of it. She's probably fucking shit up like she's trained to do. You need to move on from her anyway. In another two months, you'll be a Seraph Guardian with your wings and she'll be a distant memory. You and I both know you can't take her with you. So you might as well break it off with her."

His chocolate-colored eyes find mine, and I see the fury behind them. "Alpha, don't be a fucking asshole. I love her. Just like you love Lark. Forbidden fucking love, I know. Now get off your hypocritical high horse and help me find her. Lovenia loves me too. She says that if I take Corson's offer—"

Omega's words are cut off by the screams of Lovenia from across the hall.

"Fucking Pedro," he snarls and takes off in a sprint.

Holy shit.

The Reaper.

"Omega!" I call after him. Dammit, it's a fucking setup—I just know it.

While running after him, I get a glimpse of him as he hauls ass out the front door. I chase after him and make it into the hallway just in time to see him kick Pedro's door in and rush inside.

"Omega!" I roar again as I bolt toward Pedro's broken door. I have to stop this.

When I enter the apartment, the living room is empty and I hear another scream from Lovenia in the bedroom. Omega is just slipping inside, so I hurry after him. Once I reach the doorway, I stare in shock at the scene.

Pedro grunts as he fucks Lovenia. Both of them are butt-ass naked. Love's lips are parted in what appears to be ecstasy. Omega just gapes at them in surprise, his emotions in utter confusion.

As if on cue, Love's eyes fill with tears and she screeches out in horror. "Omega! Help me!"

Omega's body tenses up as a furious scream tears from his throat.

"What the fuck, Lovenia?" Pedro questions in bewilderment.

But it's too late. Omega's inner wild lion has been released and he pounces. "I will kill you, motherfucker!"

Lovenia scratches and pushes at Pedro, which only fuels Omega's rage as he tackles Pedro right off her. Both men hit the floor on the other side of the bed with a heavy thud.

"He raped me!" Love hisses through her tears and points in accusation at Pedro.

I stare at her, openmouthed, in disbelief, at her blatant lies. Then the sickening crunch of flesh against flesh startles me and I burst over to them.

"Omega, stop!" I attempt to pull him off Pedro by his shoulders.

He swings back and connects his elbow with my jaw, causing me to fall backwards, away from them. Before I hit the floor, I gather my bearings and leap back toward them.

"He hurt me! Pedro hurt me! Kill him, Omega!" Lovenia taunts from the bed.

As I once again try to grab Omega, who is landing one powerful punch after the other on Pedro's face, my eyes briefly find Love, who is watching with fucking glee. That bitch used my best friend. He was her assignment. She doesn't love Omega.

Finally, I seize Omega in a choke hold and haul him away from Pedro. In pure desperation, he attempts to break free from my grasp, but I hold him tighter. Hauling ass, I stumble backwards out of the bedroom with him and into the hallway.

"You asshole! Let go of me!" he garbles out as he claws at my forearm.

Ignoring him, I pull him toward the front door. I've just stepped through the broken door and into the hallway when motion to my left catches my eye. The fucking Reaper.

"Not today, weasel. Get the fuck out of here," I growl.

He shakes his head and then nods toward the stairwell.

And then it all fucking hits the fan.

"Lark, what are you doing here?" I demand.

She's standing at the top of the stairs, her wild, dark hair looking messy from sleep. If I didn't know any better, I'd say that she was the angel. Lark's certainly beautiful enough to be one.

"I came for you. What's going on?" she questions.

Another scream from Lovenia rings out inside the apartment, and when my attention is drawn against my will from my Lark to see what the noise was about, my eyes meet the wild ones of Pedro. He raises his Glock and aims it right at Omega's chest.

No!

My knee-jerk reaction is to turn with my best friend in my arms. Then I hear the blast of the gun and immediately feel the impact in the side of my ribs.

“That motherfucker!” Omega snarls as he finally breaks free from my now weak grasp.

I watch in horror as my best friend charges Pedro so fast that the idiot never has a chance to defend himself. Omega wrestles the gun with ease from Pedro’s grasp and points the weapon at his forehead.

“Don’t do it!” I choke out as I feel the tiny arms of Lark wrap around my middle, her cheek against my back.

Omega looks up at Lovenia in the doorway, who just nods her approval. Without any more hesitation, he empties the rest of the rounds into the head of Pedro.

“You’ve been shot!” Lark sobs against my back.

When she lifts her hands in front of me, they’re covered with blood. My blood. The room spins, and I stumble backwards. I see the flash of the Reaper as he pushes past us and into the apartment to collect the dark soul of Pedro.

“I’m so sorry, Lark.” My words are gasps, and I can barely stand on my own two feet.

We stumble again, this time toward the stairwell. She circles around to my front and holds me tight, but not tight enough to stop my weight from carrying us to the top of the stairs.

Looking down at my love, I whisper, “Hang on, Twiggy. I’m taking you for a ride.”

Blackness steals my vision as we fall, but I grip her close. Each time gravity pulls at her, I twist and turn, breaking her fall with my own body. My own bones break with the individual slam of every step just so that she’ll be protected. I cocoon her with my love and what little strength I have left. And when my head finally slaps onto the floor at the bottom, I know it’s done.

My time with her is over.

’Til death.

I just didn’t realize it would be this soon.

“Lar,” I murmur, but my sweet girl is limp in my arms. “Lark!” I try to scream, but the heaviness in my chest makes it sound like bubbles.

With each blink, the world spins until I'm watching my body from across the room. What the fuck is going on? Lark seems so tiny lying on top of my unmoving body, her fingers gripping my shirt.

Am I dead?

"She's going to be okay, Alpha," a familiar voice comforts me from somewhere nearby. I can't look away from her, though, to find out who is speaking to me.

"How do you know?" I ask. My voice is unfamiliar to me now. Nothing makes sense anymore.

"I'm her guardian angel, also known as Clarence, SG."

Clarence.

Clarence.

Homeless Clarence?"

"I love her," I tell him with tears in my eyes. "I will miss her so much."

He chuckles, and the warmth of it soothes my soul just a bit. "I know you do, son. But don't worry. You won't miss her."

Anger wells in my chest at his words. Of course I'll miss her. I'll miss her until the end of time.

But my thoughts are interrupted when Luc and Corson step into the foyer of the building. Both men walk over to Lark and the body of me. When Luc nudges my head with his toe, I roar at him.

"Leave us alone!" I scream.

But neither of the men turns around.

"They can't hear you, son. Don't waste your breath. You don't belong to them."

Movement in the stairwell catches my eye, and I see The Reaper descending the stairs, dragging Pedro by the neck. I know it isn't the human form of Pedro though—it's his soul. No matter how hard Pedro tries to escape, he won't. His destiny is in Hell.

"Good job," Luc praises the Reaper as he passes.

The Reaper nods and disappears with Pedro in tow.

Seconds later, a despondent-looking Omega plunks down the steps on the arm of a very pleased Lovenia.

That bitch.

"And you, Love," Luc beams at her. "You went above and beyond the call of duty. Here, you wrangled us one of the best out there. You'll be getting rewarded beyond your wildest dreams, sugar." Then he turns his attention to my best friend. "Welcome to the team, Omega. By murdering your final assignment, you skipped the ranks of Reaper and we welcome you as a Leviathan."

Lovenia releases him to hop over Lark and my body. Meanwhile, Omega stares with longing at us before raising his sad eyes to Luc and Corson.

"What happens to Alpha?" he questions as he steps over us.

Luc grumbles. "Forget about him now. He made his bed, and now, he has to lie in it. We certainly don't want him over at HEL. I'm sure HEA will figure out something to do with his ass."

With a jovial slap on Omega's shoulder, Corson chuckles. "Come on. I want to take you to your suite. You're going to love working for us. We've already prepped your room. I've sent two sexy-as-sin women to welcome you properly."

Omega growls and snaps his attention to Corson. "I don't want women. I want her." He points right at Love.

Lovenia's cheeks redden, but she looks down at her feet. "Omega, you can't have me. You were my job. You're with us now, but we will never be together."

"But I love you," he whispers.

Luc shakes his head in disapproval at him as he holds out a hand to Lovenia. Without hesitation, she takes it. With a wink, he raises it to his lips and kisses it fondly.

"Love isn't an emotion we have over at HEL. You may have feelings of lust for sweet Lovenia, just like I do, but you can't love her. Besides, who could love someone who betrayed them? You do realize, Omega, that she used you, right? You were a pawn in her game to recruit you. But don't worry. We'll take care of you. You don't need her. We have other plans for a fierce man like you."

Omega raises his gaze to Lovenia and pleads with his eyes. "Is this true, Love? I mean nothing to you?"

Lovenia bites her lip and looks down at the floor. "It is true. You were a job."

Something in Omega's eyes hardens as he turns them to Luc. "Then by all means, boss. Lead the way."

Corson grins with pride at Omega. "You're one of us now."

Omega growls out his response. "Make it four women. I'm in a mood to fuck."

Luc and Corson exchange pleased glances as they guide Omega out of the building with a seemingly lost Lovenia behind them. I hope she feels remorse for what she's done to my best friend.

"It isn't fair," I mutter to Clarence.

His warm hand settles on my shoulder. "Omega will be okay. Don't worry about him."

I'm about to tell him that his answer isn't good enough. I want to run after my best friend. I want to climb back into my body and hold Lark against me. But I can't do any of those things.

I'm stuck. Staring ahead.

I'm shaken from my thoughts when Lark moans and Clarence walks over to her.

"Is she okay?" I manage to mumble.

Clarence looks over his shoulder and grins. At first, I think he's looking at me, but his gaze falls behind me. When I smell the cigar, I know that Pallas is here. He's come for me. I should feel terror or remorse, but all I feel is grateful that it's over.

"Time to go, Alpha," Pallas booms behind me.

"Clarence, just tell me she's okay," I call out through my tears.

He smiles so beautifully that I feel it warm every part of my being. "She's okay. And so is your baby."

My baby?

She's pregnant?

"What?"

"Congrats, Daddy. I'm sorry you have to go, but I'll take care of them forever. I promise," Clarence vows as he strokes Lark's hair.

After one last glance at my sweet love, I finally turn and meet my destiny head on.

Goodbye, Lark Miller.

As I sit in the cold chair in the stark, white room, waiting for the verdict of what will happen to me, I try to imagine a life with Lark. A life where we could be a family. Her, me, and our baby.

When Pallas brought me back to HEA, he told me the truth—that my life would soon be over. He revealed that Mathias and Father Lester had explained everything to upper management, but rules were still rules.

Fornication. Voluntary sexual intercourse between two unmarried persons or two persons not married to each other. In biblical terms—idolatry. But it wasn't just the act itself that was the problem. As Minders, we're allowed to be sexual creatures if we so choose. Just not with our assignments. With each other is fine—even with those over at HEL like Omega was doing with Lovenia. That wasn't frowned upon. But with your assignment?

That was the big, fat rule I'd broken.

My thoughts dissipate when the door cracks open and Pallas steps in. His face is unreadable, and my chest feels tight. To rid myself of the anxiety, I close my eyes for a brief moment and conjure up an image of my beautiful Lark.

"Alpha," he murmurs as he approaches.

With reluctance, I open my eyes but straighten my back to face my consequences like a man. "Sir."

"After much deliberation and pulling apart your file, they've come to a conclusion," he says.

Another ache seizes my chest and to ease it, I press my palm to it. God, I miss her.

"Things are very complicated, son," he sighs, "but you didn't break any damn rules."

My brows rise in question. "That's great news, Pallas, right? But I still don't understand."

Pallas sighs and crosses his arms. "There's an internal investigation going on. We have a major problem within the organization. Someone with their own agendas has been tampering with files. We will continue to work diligently until we find the source. Unfortunately, though, your files were tampered with as well."

I look at him in question.

"Do you remember your name?" he asks.

Connor. Last time I uttered the word, I nearly lost Lark.

"No," I lie.

He rolls his eyes at me. "Lying's a sin, Connor."

I swallow the lump in my throat. "Pallas?"

"Yes, son?"

"Am I *her* Connor?"

Instead of answering me, he slaps his palm to my forehead, and I begin to feel all of my thoughts and memories disappear. I'm powerless against him when my body becomes lighter and an empty darkness fills my head. Soon, everything fades and I feel much like I did upon waking in HEA that first day—the day where my life as Alpha began.

"Goodbye, Alpha."

Epilogue

Lark

WARM SUNSHINE ON my skin wakes me from my slumber, but I can't seem to open my eyes. My whole body aches, especially my back. Was it the fall down the stairs?

Alpha!

Each eyelid feels like it weighs ten pounds as I attempt to lift them. When I finally open them, I'm confused. Am I in a hospital?

The window facing me reveals a green yard, and I spy a swing set.

Where am I?

Dragging my line of sight from the window, I look over at the wall in front of me. Someone stenciled a part of an Edgar Allan Poe poem on it—Annabel Lee, to be exact.

But our love it was stronger by far than the love
Of those who were older than we—
Of many far wiser than we—
And neither the angels in Heaven above
Nor the demons down under the sea
Can ever dissever my soul from the soul
Of the beautiful Annabel Lee

So beautiful.

A noise from the bedside table startles me—singing coming from a baby monitor. An angel singing, I think. As the sweet voice of a girl begins singing "Jesus Loves Me," a tear rolls out of my eye.

Who is the sweet girl singing?

Three framed photos sit behind the baby monitor. A familiar ultrasound picture. My baby.

Am I in Heaven?

Beside it is a picture of Connor and me on our wedding day.

I'm most certainly in Heaven.

The third picture confuses me. A family.

My family.

My green eyes shine happily as I hold the hand of a little girl no more than six years old as she sits on the shoulders of a certain blond-haired, blue-eyed man. *Connor Miller.*

Reaching over, I snatch the picture up and bring it close to my face to inspect it. The picture is perfection. If this is Heaven, I never want to leave.

Please, God. Don't make me leave.

I run my thumb across the picture to see if it's real. The glass feels cold. Hard. Real. Then a hand slides over my bare belly and I freeze.

No.

I don't even want to imagine who could be under the blanket beside me. But as the thumb strokes my stomach, I know. God, do I ever know.

"Good morning, Connor," I whisper as silent tears stream down. "I've missed you so much."

He lifts his head from under the blanket and grins a goofy smile at me. "What? You missed this morning breath?" he laughs as he attacks my lips with his.

His taste.

His smell.

His skin.

All Connor.

My Connor.

A sob pierces the air, and he sits up, alarmed, narrowing his blue eyes at me.

"You're crying. What's wrong? Don't blame it on pregnancy hormones again. Are you hungry? I'll make you some food."

Pregnancy hormones?

I rub a hand over my barely swollen belly. "I'm pregnant?"

His eyes dart back and forth between mine as he attempts to understand what's going on in my head. Then he purses his lips together in concern but nods.

My eyes fall to my bare chest and belly. The star tattoos are gone. The sweet, pink bow tattoo is gone.

I'm in Heaven for sure.

"Lar, you're scaring me. What's going on in that head of yours?" Connor questions.

His eyes are so blue. My mind briefly remembers the ones so black, and I close my eyes.

"Nothing, Connor. Everything will be just fine. I love you," I tell him with a smile as I reopen my eyes.

He beams at me and lowers his body over mine, this time kissing me with slow reverence. Is this what Clarence meant? That I would be with my family again? I know I didn't dream everything—the deaths of Connor and my baby, Alpha finding me, and eventually losing him. *It was real.*

"I'm going to make love to my gorgeous, pregnant wife," Connor murmurs between kisses.

The room spins at the prospect of having my husband back.

I nod my head in slow agreement and he doesn't hesitate before pushing himself into me. My eyes black out from the pleasure, and all I see are stars.

Six beautiful stars.

"You're a star, Lar. I love you so much," Connor breathes against my lips as he makes love to me.

"I love you too, big boy."

My body feels like a live wire—full of electricity—as my orgasm slices through me. This orgasm doesn't belong to me though. It belongs to us. Connor groans as he joins in on an orgasm shared by two people—two married lovers who own the key to each other's souls.

And what about Alpha?

Alpha is in there somewhere. I'll never let go of that piece of him inside me.

"I could stay here all day making love to you, woman, but someone has to feed our daughter," Connor chuckles as he climbs off me.

I close my eyes as I hear him pad off to the bathroom. Our daughter. That will never get old.

"Mommy!" a sweet voice chirps from the doorway.

Heaven.

My eyes jerk open and I look over at the blond-haired, green-eyed little girl in the doorway. A perfect mix of Connor and me. I pull the covers up over my chest as she runs around to my side of the bed.

"Give Mommy a hug," I smile.

When her small arms wrap around my neck, I want to melt. I love this little girl, even if I don't know her name. She's mine. My daughter.

"I love you, Mommy."

"I love you too, sweetie."

"Al and I are going to have Oreos for breakfast. Lark, you should eat something healthy for the baby."

Al.

Alpha.

He's here!

Relieved tears fill spill over, but I'm confused.

"Alysson," Connor instructs, "why don't you go pour us some milk?"

She releases me and with excitement bounds out of the room.

Alysson is Al.

A pain aches in my heart, but I try to push it away.

Connor watches me from the doorway of the bathroom. He's wearing a pair of pajama pants now, but he still hasn't put a shirt on. The man is handsome as ever, and I've missed him so much. But then I notice a scar on his ribs and stare at him in puzzlement.

"Where'd you get the scar?" I demand.

His brows rise playfully as he smirks at me. "Would you believe a Mexican gangster shot me?" he jokes.

"Daddy, I spilled some!" Alysson shrieks from the kitchen.

When he turns away from me to stride toward the bedroom door, I die. I seriously die when I see his back.

The most beautiful angel wings are tattooed over the muscles there. Wings *I* gave to him.

"Alpha," I barely whisper with my hand over my mouth.

My blond-haired husband looks over his shoulder, and I swear his blue eyes are almost black.

"Time for breakfast, Twiggy." He winks.

Before he leaves the room, I call out to him. "Wait!"

He turns my way once more with a brow raised in question.

"Are we in Heaven, big boy?"

His smile is so beautiful that it lights up the entire room. "No, but this sure is close."

The End.

A Note from the Author

I hope you enjoyed Alpha & Omega.
To us authors, reviews matter.
Please consider leaving a review.
Thanks a bunch!

Omega & Love

Coming Soon . . .

Chapter One

Omega

Six months after joining HEL Enterprises . . .

"HARDER, OMEGA!" VIV screams as I pound into her from behind.

This chick is all woman. Curvy hips. Full lips that can work magic on a cock—my cock in particular. Blond hair ripe for pulling. She's a sexual beast, but she still can't keep up with my ongoing carnal needs. She's a champ for trying. I'll definitely keep her around for a while longer.

I slap her white ass hard and smirk at the red handprint that immediately begins to color her flesh.

"I'm coming!" she cries out.

After grabbing a handful of blond hair, I roughly yank her head back. "Not yet, baby."

She whimpers, but I feel her relax the walls of her pussy and let go of the orgasm she wanted so badly to give in to. To reward her for her obeying, I reach to her front and begin massaging her clit as if I've been doing it my whole life.

"Please, Omega," she begs as her sweaty body rocks against mine.

I groan when I feel curls of pleasure deep from within me. I guess I'll I grant her wish. "Now," I bark and jerk once again on her hair.

"Oh, God!" she moans as her body quivers wildly, finally giving in to her need for me.

The way her pussy squeezes my cock sends my orgasm pumping into her. I thrust a few more times and revel in the way my balls slap her bare pussy. This woman feels damn good. Almost as good as the one who will be here later.

When I pop her on the ass once more for good measure, she slides off of me and purrs over her shoulder, "You're amazing."

I laugh at her words as she crawls away from me and lies down on her back on the bed. With her blond, curly hair spread around her on the black, satin sheets, she looks every bit a Playboy model. Huge tits quiver with each overexerted breath she takes, and her flat stomach begs to be licked.

"Don't get too comfortable, Viv," I grin. "Lacey is coming by in an hour. You know how she feels about threesomes. Time to skedaddle."

Viv's big, blue eyes widen like saucers. "Omega . . . I thought you and I were something special. We fuck just about every day. I think that's pretty incredible. Dare I say it's love?" she teases.

I freeze at her words.

Love.

The vilest word in the English language. It also happens to be the name of the Devil's favorite plaything—the woman who crushed my soul.

I hate love.

I hate Love.

Fury glides through my veins like a rush of heroin. "Get the fuck out and don't come back."

"What?" she asks in shock as she sits up. Her lips form a pout, and if I weren't so fucking pissed right now, I'd bite the bottom one.

"Don't make me say it again, baby."

She stares at me with hurt-filled eyes as I climb off the bed. Then I shake my head at her and storm toward the bathroom.

Over my shoulder, I spit out, "Viv, when you leave, don't come back. I'm tired of your skanky ass. You bore the hell out of me."

A shocked gasp is the last thing I hear before I slam the door shut.

* * *

"Someone has their panties in a wad," Gabe taunts loudly with a grin as I enter the bar and stride toward him.

I flip him off as I slide into the booth across from him. This is one of the things I love about HEL. We get to pretty much do whatever the fuck we want. There are no rules. Rules were made for breaking. As long as we do what's for the good of the company, they reward us with whatever our heart desires. And tonight, I desire a Jack and Coke shared with a friend.

"I go commando, remember?" I smirk as he pushes my drink over to me.

We met not long after I moved over to HEL. His suite is beside mine, and we've been known to throw a couple of kickass parties.

"Don't remind me. I'd like to forget that tan ass of yours. But seriously, how is your ass that tan? Do you have a tanning bed in your room? I'll tell Corson to order me one. I deserve it," he says smugly.

I fight the laughter that threatens to burst from me as I remember the night he got a glimpse of my ass. That night, I was balls-deep in hot, black-skinned model who was visiting from Nairobi. The woman had shorter hair than I do but was a wild beast in bed. Gabe burst through the door thinking someone was getting murdered only to see my ass clench as I came all over her back.

"Your albino ass would burn," I chuckle before I sip my liquor.

He scoffs at me. "Shut up, asshole, and stop calling me an albino."

"Man, your skin's as white as snow. Where are your seven dwarves?"

This time, he flips me off.

"Uh oh," he groans. "Viv just walked in."

Earlier, before I texted him to meet me at the bar on the fifth floor of our building, I briefly explained to him about what she'd said. He knows how much I hate Love and what that word does to me. I could barely stay hard for "Loves to Lick" Lacey. She ended up sucking me off and then leaving shortly after.

"Is she coming over here?" I question, staring into my glass.

"No, she's walking over to a table of guys. But fuck, we need to leave," he says urgently.

The moment he utters out his words, I know. I know exactly why we need to leave.

Lovenia.

I can feel her presence before I even see her. She's magnetic like that, and I fucking hate that about her. From all the way over here, her seductive perfume twists and curls through the air toward me like wild tendrils of ivy. I'm enveloped in her scent, and I want to puke.

"Shit. She's walking over here," Gabe curses under his breath.

Gabe's a good friend, and I'm pretty sure he'd do anything for me. I trust him even if he does look like a fucking vampire. His dark hair dips down in a widow's peak on his forehead, and his eyebrows are perpetually furrowed as if he always means to scowl. He could pass for fucking Dracula, but the man is harmless. Loyal. And funny as hell.

"Why the fuck is she coming over here? Didn't the bitch get the message? We're over. If I recall, she's the one who made that call six months ago," I growl.

Gabe sympathetically shakes his head but turns on the sugary, fake charm when she reaches our table. "Sweet Love, so nice seeing you here. Where's your boyfriend?"

She clicks her tongue in annoyance. "You mean your boss? Luc's in his office. And he's not my boyfriend. I just please him when he needs it."

"Him and everyone else," Gabe murmurs loud enough for only me to hear.

"What's that, Edward?" she snaps.

I stifle a laugh at her vampire reference—not because it isn't funny, but because she doesn't deserve my laughter. She deserves nothing from me. I won't even fucking look at her. I'm about to pass out from holding my breath so I don't have to smell her intoxicating scent.

"Omega, Luc wants to see you," Lovenia mutters cautiously to me. It's the first time she's spoken directly to me since she told me that she'd used me for her own personal gain. Her voice, like before, winds its way through my core and niggles at my heart.

I hate her voice.

"About what?" I grumble as I eyeball a piece of ice in my glass.

An exaggerated sigh rushes from her, but I ignore it and wait for her to continue. She doesn't need me to look at her to tell me what he needs.

"Fine. Be a child. He wants to talk about your next assignment. In fact, he wants to talk to the both of us. Together."

This time, I do look at her. Her perfectly manicured hand rests on her cocked-to-the-side hip—a hip I held on to many nights as I made love to her body. I hate that hip.

Finally, I drag my gaze along the swell of her luscious tits in her fitted, red dress, all the way up to her brown eyes. One of her eyebrows is raised as she waits for an answer.

"No."

Her nostrils flare angrily as she shrieks, "No is not an answer you're allowed to give! You've been summoned. With me. Whether you like it or not. Now get your big ass out of that booth and follow me."

I slam my drink down on the table and slide out of the booth. Once I'm standing, I tower over her curvy frame. She lifts her chin in faux bravery and glares at me. I hate myself because I have the urge to taste those perfect lips of hers. Those same lips that made promises her heart never kept.

Stepping forward until my chest brushes against hers, I look down into her mocha-colored eyes. She smells so goddamned good. Before I do something stupid, I press a finger against her chest bone and push her away from me. Her eyes widen at the fact that I touched her, but she quickly schools away her surprise.

"You, Love"—I point in her face—"Don't have the luxury of telling me what to do anymore. Your lying ass can follow me to go see Luc, not the other way around. And please don't talk to me unless you absolutely must because you fucking disgust me."

With that, I briefly meet the nod of approval from Gabe before turning on my heel and stalking away from her. The click of her heels following behind me lets me know she understands the rules.

God, I hate her.

Take Me to Church—Hozier
Run—Snow Patrol
Heart Heart Head—Meg Myers
Cupid Carries a Gun—Marilyn Manson
Adelaide—Meg Myers
3 Libras—A Perfect Circle
Crazy—Gnarls Barkley
Monster—Meg Myers
Going to Hell—The Pretty Reckless
Go—Meg Myers
Surprise—Filter
The Noose—A Perfect Circle
It's Just You—Filter

Books by Author K Webster

The Breaking the Rules Series:
Broken (Book 1)—Available Now!
Wrong (Book 2)—Available Now!
Scarred (Book 3)—Available Now!
Mistake (Book 4)—Available Now!
Crushed (Book 5—a novella)—Coming Soon!

The Vegas Aces Series:
Rock Country (Book 1)—Available Now!
Rock Heart (Book 2)—Available Now!
Rock Bottom (Book 3)—Available Now!
Rock Out (Book 4)—Coming Soon!

Alpha & Omega—Available Now!
Omega & Love—Coming Soon!

Apartment 2B (Standalone Novel)—Available Now!
Love and Law (Standalone Novel)—Available Now!
Moth to a Flame (Standalone Novel)—Available Now!
Erased (Standalone Novel)—Available Now!
The Road Back to Us (Standalone Novel)—Coming Soon!

Acknowledgements

A big thank you goes out to my husband, Matt. This story paid homage to our endless, timeless love. You'll always be my Alpha—the inspiration for all of my stories. You're my walking thesaurus, my sounding board, and my biggest supporter. I love you, honey.

I want to thank the beta readers on this book, whom are also my friends. Nikki McCrae, Anne Jolin, Wendy Colby, Dena Marie, Elizabeth Thiele, Lori Christensen, Michelle Ramirez, Shannon Martin, Amy Bosica, Holly Sparks, Sian Davies, and Elizabeth Clinton, you guys provided AMAZING feedback. You all gave helpful ideas to make the story better and gave me incredible encouragement. I appreciate all of your comments and suggestions.

Thank you to my sister Jennifer Berger for being my eagle eye and doing one final read through to catch any mistakes that snuck in even after being through the editor and reading it a bazillion times.

I'm especially thankful for the Breaking the Rules Babes. You ladies are amazing with your support and friendship. When I hear about catty and nasty street teams, I chuckle. I know our group is nothing but sweet, loving women that care for one another. I'm truly blessed to have you all in my life!

Mickey, my fabulous editor from I'm a Book Shark, thank you for once again being the bomb at what you do. I totally and irrevocably thank you for PULLING my attention to every lovely adverb in my manuscript. If you were here, I'd SLIDE my arm around you and tightly squeeze you to me. And yes, once again, TEARS WILL FILL MY EYES. Hey Mickey, you're so fine, you're so fine you blow my mind—hey Mickey! Love ya!

Thank you Stacey Blake for working your gorgeous magic and for being such a great wino friend. Love you!

Thank you so much Nicole from IndieSage Promotions for helping whip my marketing into shape . . . you create some beautiful graphics and I'm so grateful that you help me!

Lastly but certainly not least of all, thank you to all of the wonderful readers out there that are willing to hear my story and enjoy my characters like I do. It means the world to me!

I'm a thirty three year old self-proclaimed book nerd. Married to my husband for eleven years, we enjoy spending time with our two lovely children. Writing is a newly acquired fun hobby for me that has now turned into a livelihood over the past year. In the past, I've enjoyed the role as a reader. However, I have learned I absolutely love taking on the creative role as the writer. Something about determining how the story will play out intrigues me to no end.

This writing experience has been a blast and I've met some really fabulous people along the way. I hope my readers enjoy reading my stories as much as I do writing them. I look forward to connecting with you all!

Join K Webster's newsletter to receive a couple of updates a month on new releases and exclusive content. To join, all you need to do is go here (http://eepurl.com/9AqRD).

Facebook
https://www.facebook.com/authorkwebster
Blog
http://authorkwebster.wordpress.com/
Twitter
https://twitter.com/KristiWebster
Email
kristi@authorkwebster.com
Goodreads
https://www.goodreads.com/user/show/10439773-k-webster
Instagram
http://instagram.com/kristiwebster

Made in the USA
Middletown, DE
09 January 2022

58271804R00118